ON A ROLL

A NEW COLLECTION OF MEMORIES AND IMAGININGS

BY 15 WICHITA, KANSAS AREA SENIOR AUTHORS

ALL PROCEEDS OF THIS BOOK GO TO
SENIOR SERVICES INC. OF WICHITA, KS
A NOT-FOR-PROFIT CHARITY.

2022 © Starla Enterprises, Inc.

All rights reserved. No part of this publication may be reproduced, stored in a retrieval system, or transmitted in any form or by any means without prior written permission of the publisher or by the individual authors, except by a reviewer who may quote brief passages in a review to be printed in a newspaper, magazine, or journal. Individual authors retain copyright for their work.

For information regarding permission, write to Starla Enterprises, Inc.
Attention: Permissions Department,
740 W. 2nd, Ste. 200, Wichita, KS 67203

First Edition

ISBN: 978-1-0879-6171-2

Editor & Cover Design by Starla Criser

Printed in the U.S.A.

About Our Project

Starla Criser started this project in 2017. The continuing project focuses on publishing writing collections from members of the Wichita, Kansas senior centers. The idea came after working with excited members of the writing classes she offers, starting in 2016.

The classes started as teaching older adults about some pieces and parts of writing in its many facets. Programs included everything from what is a genre, to types of writing, to all the basics of a project's creation, all the way to publishing and marketing.

Having published over 100 projects in several ways since 1999, she has observed and experienced a lot of the good and bad things in a writer's career. She wanted to share what she had learned, as well as learn from what her students shared with her of their own experiences.

Over the years, the classes have progressed from teaching to being more of a shared learning and networking style. There are still helpful skill programs presented, as well as other facets in the vast writing world. Students share projects they are working on and share their attempt at trying out the challenging writing exercises. A number of those exercise results are included in the anthologies.

Write On, published in 2017, is a collection of stories, memoirs, and poems from 23 Wichita area authors.

Write Again, published in 2018, is a collection of stories, articles, memoirs, and poems from 29 Wichita area authors.

Daring to Share, published in 2019, is a collection of poetry, thoughts, and short stories from 35 Wichita area authors.

All the collections are available online at Barnes & Noble and Amazon. They are also in the Wichita library.

CONTENTS

Inspirational

Memories

CONTRIBUTORS

Writing Challenges

Many of the authors in this collection belong to a group of senior adults who get together monthly for writing classes, to network, and to support each other. Some authors have used part of the exercises we do in the creation of their project(s). See if you can figure out who used the exercises and which ones. The words do not all have to be used or can be used in another form.

WORDS: envelopes – stinky – boots – peaches - puppies

POETRY PROMPT: Use the words should – would – could

WORDS: TV – orange – goose – sandals - stubby
PROMPT: Write about a meal or dinner going horribly wrong.

WORDS: scissors – mustard – monkey – tutu – bushy
PROMPT: Write about getting lost at a carnival or festival.

WORDS: zipper – tomato – goldfish – hat - fat

WORDS: pillow – pickles – porcupine – pink
PROMPT: Start with "This is my worst nightmare..."

WORDS: desk – hamburger – soccer – sweet - flamingo

WORDS: glue – strawberry – penguin – slippers – giggle
PROMPT: Write about being in a talent show.

WORDS: paperclip – yogurt – buffalo – tie – skinny
PROMPT: Write about accepting a dare.

WORDS: museum – lemon – eagle – truck – blue

THOUGHTS ABOUT LIFE

Um, Um Good!

Don Boldea

I'm a typical college male. I don't know how to cook, anything! As a bachelor, I eat out a lot. Okay, I do have, besides beer and milk in the fridge, Cocoa Puffs cereal in the cabinet, TV dinners and cheese pizzas in the freezer. Oh yea, I forgot, there are all of those important snacks on the counter along with a healthy bowl of greenish oranges. It's all you need when the guys are over to watch the game: basketball, football, baseball, golf, and all of the other games that start or end with ball.

When I date, I always take her to a nice restaurant for a romantic dinner. However, on the first day of a new semester class, International Relationships, I sat next to an international, smell good, very attractive female student.

Before the class started, I introduced myself. She was certainly beautiful and as we talked, I knew that I had met someone very special. Our conversation was cut short when the stubby professor began his lecture. After class, with some trepidation of rejection, I pulled up from the depths of my well-worn sandals all of my courage and asked if she would have dinner with me to finish our conversation. She accepted.

We hit it off straight away. After a dozen or so dates and eating at all of the nice restaurants I could afford, she said that she would like to cook me a very special dinner. Boy was that good news. My monthly food allowance ran out three months ago.

Corina was not only beautiful, but she was intelligent, interesting and she was a great cook, as I would find out. The evening finally came for her tasty gourmet Hungarian dinner. I brought a bottle of Bull's Blood; Corina said it was the perfect and beloved Hungarian wine for every meal.

First there were appetizers, next a salad, three main entrees, followed by dessert and several glasses of wine. I was ready for a long winter's nap, all helped by a slight buzz from the many glasses of that very hearty wine.

We talked for hours about our plans after graduation. When the evening finally ended, I thanked her for a wonderful dinner and conversation. Before I turned for the door and with much anticipation, I gave her my best thank you kiss. Then, I said something very stupid. "I would like to cook my mother's special dish for you." Without hesitation, she said yes. I was close to passing out when I realized what I had asked and how quickly she said yes.

After our goodnights, I ran to my apartment, closed, and locked the door. It was late when I called my mother and asked her for the recipe for our family's favorite roast goose. After she laughed for a moment or two, she asked if I was feeling well. She knew that I not only didn't like roasted goose, but that I didn't know how to cook anything but microwave pizza. Her hearty laugh started again.

Long story made longer, I bought the ingredients, followed to the word my mom's recipe and her instructions for baking the goose and plating it. Side dishes included sweet potatoes and sautéed zucchini with herb spices. Finally, I purchased a bottle of a good California vineyard, Pinot Noir.

The apartment was filled with various aromas when she arrived. I opened the door and immediately her nose wrinkled a bit as the wall of unique aromas slapped her in the face. This was the first sign; dinner wasn't going to be a proud moment for me.

I took her hand and led her out to the balcony for some fresh air, apologized and admitted that I wasn't a cook. No, I wouldn't have made Mom very proud of me. What do I do now? She knew my embarrassment and very tactfully consoled me. How could a horribly bad meal have gone even more horrible?

I finally looked at her. "Would you like a seven top frozen microwaved pizza from a box, served with a subtle Pinot Noir?"

"Oh yes," she said, "I would love a seven topped frozen microwaved pizza from a box, served with Pinot Noir! That's my favorite dish. Um, um good!"

We both laughed and spent the rest of the evening on the balcony under the stars.

The Old Mill

R. Tobey

Under a leafy canopy
It sits old and worn,
Shadows make a quiet place
Where memories are born.

Here the river flows silently
Along a sandy shore
And there is the ancient mill wheel
That will turn no more.

It slumbers away softly
Here in this sleepy space,
A post card picture from the past;
A perfect resting place.

The old mill at Oxford, Kansas was built in 1874 to use water power from the Arkansas River.

The Crash
Coe Holden

A story of two friends: Jake Jackson, J.J., and John Johnston, J.J.

It was a nice fall morning when my friend Jake Jackson called and asked me to go for an airplane ride. He just had his plane tuned up and gone over to make sure it was airworthy.

I met him at the airport at about ten the next morning. He said it is all fueled up and we could take off as soon as he filed a flight plan. He did the run up and checked all he was supposed to before we started.

The tower said we could get to the runway and Jake gave it full throttle and soon we were airborne. We were soon over a wooded area and the trees were turning colors. Then with no warning, the engine sputtered one, then started running okay.

Jake said we must turn back.

An hour passed and suddenly the prop just stopped, and all the gauges went to zero. Even the radio went dead. No way to call for help now.

Jake said to look for a clearing in case we needed one in a hurry. I could see the trees getting closer to us all the time.

As we were clipping the tops of some of the taller ones, Jake said to get ready for a crash.

I ducked down as far as I could behind the windshield, and I could see the wing on my side being ripped off and fuel went everywhere. I could hear branches breaking and some of the plane being torn apart.

We crashed into a big tree with a hefty thud. We hit really hard.

Jake asked, "Are you okay?"

I said, "Not sure," because I was hurting from the seat belt. "How about you?"

He said, "I think I may have a broken arm and my leg is starting to hurt. I think it may be broken, too."

I got out as soon as I could and helped Jake unfasten his seat belt and get out of the plane. We were lucky there was not a fire. We guessed no battery power must have something to do with it.

I could see a small clearing about 50 yards ahead. Jake said to get the bag from behind the pilot's seat. It had survival gear in it.

After I got the bag, we hobbled to the clearing, and I patched us both up as good as I could. Jake had a cut on his cheek, and I had a cut on my forehead. I made splints out of sticks for his leg and arm. I tied them up with vines that were growing wild.

In the bag was a short-handled ax, a shovel that was also a pick, like a G-I shovel I had seen in a store. There was also a small saw, a first aid kit, a small canvas about eight feet square, and six ready to eat meals. Not much for two people, but we were glad for what we had.

The sky was clouding over in the west. Jake said he knew of a front moving in, but he'd thought we would be back home before the weather would change. I said we had best get some kind of shelter built or find something really quick.

So, I started making a lean-to the best I could, but with the small tarp, it would not be big enough for two. I made a bigger frame with branches I cut with the saw and the ax, and then I tied them together with more vines. They seemed to be strong enough for what we needed. I started weaving some smaller branches and leaves. Soon we had somewhat of a shelter. Jake helped when he could.

Now it was raining, and I said we had better gather some firewood before it all got wet. Jake did the best he could. With the help of some maps that were in a case, and some matches I found, we soon had a small fire. We stretched out on our makeshift shelter by the fire, both hurting from the crash and the chilly dampness. We soon drifted off to sleep.

It rained most of the night, but we were dry. The next morning, we woke up to a heavy overcast sky. No use building a signal fire. We each ate one of the ready meals and knew we should look for another food source.

I went out into the woods and found a lot of berries and nuts that had fallen from the trees. This should get us by for a few days I hoped. The berries were tart and we had to crack the nuts with the shovel. We spent most of the day gathering dry wood for our fire and the signal fire. Most of the dry wood came from under fallen trees. We put the wood under the small tarp to keep it dry.

The next morning, we woke up to another cloudy day. We noticed the fog was about to our knees. We were in the clouds. No rescue this morning.

Come afternoon it started to rain again. We each had a ready meal and some tart berries and nuts. I went to gather more berries and nuts and saw where a bear had been there. Now there was something else to be concerned about. I didn't see the bear so we guessed it went on to better riper berries.

We spent most of the day just sleeping the best we could. We were hurting a lot but alive. Thankful for that.

The next morning, we saw the sun rise and thought this might be a good day. We ate the last of our ready meals and started the signal fire. We put some evergreen branches on the fire to make a lot of smoke, hoping someone would see us.

We kept the fire going all morning, and about noon, we heard a plane heading our way. We saw it and started waving our arms and the tarp, but the plane just flew over and disappeared.

Soon it came back, lower this time, and went on. Our hopes were low. Did they see us or not?

An hour or so passed, then we heard a helicopter. It landed in the small clearing; it had a Medevac name on the side. Two men got out and checked us over. They had us gather our gear and soon we were off to where we could get medical attention. I think we both will be okay.

If I ever go in a small aircraft again. I will make sure the survival gear is there.

North-west Kansas

R. Tobey sketches

Near Salina, Kansas

Alamo Cottonwood Genus Populas
Ghost Ranch, Abiquiu, New Mexico
Sherry A. Phillips

Golden leaf clusters clatter

A restless rustle

Dancing with soft windy whispers

On sun warmed days then

Faint when winter gusts

Through gnarled arms

With elbow twists.

Sentry

Along the beat down path

To Canyon of the Saints

Trod by seekers

Of wisdom, peace, and rest.

I am traveler on that road

Bent over but looking up to pure blue sky reverie

That trumpets me home.

The Fishing Story
Coe Holden

This is a story about a man named Fred Wilson. Fred works for a large corporation as an accountant and has for many years. He dresses in an expensive shirt and tie every day. His shoes are shined, and he doesn't like to have any dirt on him. He has no hobbies and very few friends. On the weekends, he just mostly watches TV because he works hard all week. He likes to watch fishing shows and the pros who catch fish. It seems like every cast catches a big fish. He thinks that would be a good way to relax.

So, Fred goes to a sporting goods store to buy stuff needed to go fishing. At the store, he senses the salesman knows he can make a big sale here, but Fred isn't concerned. The man shows Fred a lot of rods and tells him about the action of each rod and what it can do and sells him a real expensive rod.

Next, the salesman shows Fred some mostly expensive reels and he buys a real good one. Then comes the line, hooks, sinkers, and lures of all kinds. Fred leaves the store with everything he believes necessary to go fishing and then some.

Fred can hardly wait for the weekend so he can go out and catch a big one.

He calls up his friend Joe, who does a lot of fishing and asks where he can catch a lot of fish. Joe invites Fred to go with him the next weekend.

Early Saturday, the two of them get started early in the morning. Joe picks him up and off they go to a pond Joe knows about. Fred can hardly wait to do his first cast.

Joe helped with getting everything rigged up. When Joe opened a jar of bait, Fred almost lot his lunch. It was the most awful bad smelling stuff, so Joe used some rubber gloves to bait the hook.

Now for the big cast. Fred rears back and with a mighty heave, the line goes straight up into a tree. After some pulling, the line is loose but without the hook and sinker.

Joe helps get everything ready again, and said, "Watch me cast." He flips his line out in the perfect place.

Fred tries it, and the line goes out but only a few feet. Joe told him it might catch one there. They both sat there for what seemed like a long time. To Fred, it is next to forever.

Joe catches the first fish. It is small, so he throws it back.

Then suddenly Fred's line takes a big lunge toward the water and Joe says, "Grab your pole!"

Fred makes a grab and loses his balance and takes a big step toward the pond. Hanging on to the pole, he slips on the muddy bank and steps into the water about to belt high. There he is, holding on to the fishing pole with one hand and trying to get hold of anything he can to get him out of the water.

With Joe's help, Fred gets both feet on dry land again, but in the excitement, he steps on his new fishing pole and breaks it in half, but he lands the fish. It is a nice one and big enough to keep.

And there he stood soaking wet and muddy from head to toe.

Then they hear someone behind them say, "I am a Game Warden. Nice fish and too bad about your bad luck with your fishing pole. Let me see your fishing license."

Joe shows him his, but in the excitement of buying his fishing gear, Fred forgot to buy one. The warden writes him a ticket to appear in court.

They go home without talking. Fred is very disappointed. He gives Joe the fish and the rest of his tackle. From now on, he thinks fishing is not for him.

Windmill in a wheat field in Sumner County Kansas
(Sumner County is the nation's largest wheat producer.)

Growing Up in Kansas – Haiku
Connie Holt

Corner lot baseball

Play all day, then scared, run home

Up moon-filled alley.

Boys become sailors.

Rolling through the swaying wheat,

Ready to set sail.

"Kansas seems so flat!"

Said the traveler one day.

"Does Flint Hills sound flat?"

Fly Boys stay here as

Their U.S.A. tour is up,

Say, "It's the people!"

Looking for Something
Coe Holden

I know I had it earlier, but I can't find it.

I have looked high and low!

I know it is here someplace.

I have been the only one here. But where can it be?

I'll look again high and low, up and down and all around.

I know it is here someplace. And when I have almost given up,

It will appear almost like magic. And there it is.

I must have known it was there all the time because,

I put it there, and it is the last place I looked for it.

Forever and Ever
Starla Criser

Aggie pulled her favorite baking dish from the oven and set it on the glass cooktop. She stepped back and felt sick as she stared in horror at the sad-looking, blackened goose and unrecognizable vegetables beside it. What had gone wrong?

A glance at the stove's clock told her she was in trouble. Her new husband would return from the airport in minutes with his parents. This was their first meal together and her first chance to impress her in-laws.

With a sigh, she hung her head in disappointment. She'd seen a goose being cooked on her favorite TV cooking show, Worst Cooks in America. Maybe that should have been her first clue that this attempt could go astray. But she'd thought she could do better. Wrong.

Get over it! Figure out something else.

She raced to the refrigerator, determined to find anything to make some kind of meal. Tom didn't deserve to have a failure for a wife. Okay, he'd known that cooking wasn't her specialty. But she was a master with a microwave! And she had many restaurants on her speed dial for quick deliveries.

Opening the refrigerator door, she stared at the basically empty space. A tub of butter and a gallon of milk, probably out of date. She wasn't good with expiration dates. A couple of jars of nearly empty jams completed the contents.

Hopeful that just maybe the meat/produce drawer held something, she pulled it open. Seriously! She squinted at the partial tomato in a plastic container. Although it was hard to tell the blob was actually a tomato any longer. There was a bacon package with two pieces of what looked more like jerky than bacon. And a gorgeous orange.

Heart heavy and almost all hope to save herself gone, Aggie closed the refrigerator and hurried her way to the small pantry. Her left sandal got caught in a sticky spot on the floor, and she stumbled and smashed her stubby little toe into the corner of the stove.

She gave up, not even bothering to open the pantry door. They'd only been married two weeks, only been home from their honeymoon a week. Catching up at work had taken most of their time. When they'd finally gotten home each night, all either could manage was collapsing on their bed. Seconds after that, they'd gotten lost in each other. Food wasn't even a thought. Good thing they both grabbed a quick breakfast on the way to their respective offices and ate lunch out, too.

Tears burned her eyes, and she slid down to sit on the floor. The smell of burned goose and charred vegetables drifted down to her. She was the worst wife ever!

Aggie was in the middle of an intense personal pity party when the door opened from the garage. She didn't even have time to wipe her tears away before two strong arms reached down to pull her up. Before she could stop a final sniffle, Tom plastered her body against him, his arms holding her close.

"I made reservations at our favorite restaurant, sweetheart." He patted her back gently. "That okay with you?"

She pulled in a shuddery breath and looked up at him. His warm brown eyes mirrored love, understanding, and a hint of amusement. She was torn between wanting to kiss him for coming to her rescue or punching him in the stomach for sensing that she would have a cooking disaster.

He settled her indecision and gave her a quick kiss. It weakened her knees and destroyed her irritation.

A non-too-subtle throat clearing broke them apart. "Don't we need to be going, son?" Tom's dad asked from a few feet behind them.

Aggie groaned, and her face heated. First was the cooking disaster, and now getting caught all but climbing all over her husband.

Said husband chuckled, still holding her close to him. "We could just let the two of you go..."

This time Aggie got even with him for traumatizing her. She pushed out of his embrace, glared in annoyance at him, and glanced at his mother. "Any chance you will take him back?"

His mother's eyes flashed with amusement, and she shook her head. "Sorry. He's all yours now."

"She's right," Tom said, reaching out to caress Aggie's cheek. "I'm all yours, forever and ever. I married you for good times and bad, and for cooking wonders and disasters."

The frustration melted away at his expression's warmth and determined declaration. "Score one for 'cooking disasters.'" She smiled at her in-laws. "So, who's ready to go eat someplace with edible food?"

Lake Afton - near Wichita, Kansas

R. Tobey sketches

San Juan Forest, Colorado

Left

Connie Holt

Bobby left me here on the track,
Oh! So very long ago.
He was so proud and showed me off,
As my headlight brightly glowed.

Around and around, past every town,
The houses so very small.
In front yards children waved their hands,
Swelled with pride, I felt so tall!

Now the dust is thick and my engine's dull—
If only my Bobby would come.
Once more I'd whistle loud and clear!
And make my daily run.

After the Fiesta
Coe Holden

Summertime after the Fiesta,

It is time for a Siesta.

So, catch some ZZZZZZ.

It will put your mind at ease.

So, a quick nap will make you as sharp as a tack.

So, go ahead and lay down your head,

Be it in an easy chair or in the bed.

I have heard it said,

Rest is best for the mind.

So, lay down your head and unwind.

FUN AND HUMOR

Back In My Day!

"Yesterday All My Troubles Seemed So Far Away.
. . . Oh, I Believe in Yesterday" . . .

Don Boldea

Back in my day, there weren't such things as computers, only handwritten letters, folded, stuffed in envelopes, stamped, and placed in a mailbox.

Nor were there such things as cellular phones. Your phone stayed home where you could find it, and it didn't need to be charged up to work.

Back in my day, there weren't air conditioners. You just turned on the twelve-inch diameter, three-bladed circulating fan and suffered the hot, humid, and stinky summer days praying for the fall season to hurry up its cooler days to begin.

Of course, when winter began, and there wasn't a pair of suitable warm, dry boots to wear in the deep snow, a pair of ankle-high, high-top leather shoes did the job.

In spring, there weren't any sweet, syrupy canned peaches on the shelf in your neighborhood grocery store. You would simply pick those fresh, sweet peaches off your next-door neighbor's tree.

Back in my day, you weren't running down the street from growling, snarling, and sometimes biting dogs. Instead, you would be playing with fluffy and cute puppies that melted your heart.

Yes, that was a brief look at Back in My Day as I remember it. It was and is my Yesterday!

What's That Smell?
Marcia Helten

Debbie steps into the house and
lets the door slam behind her. Home from sch
ool at last. She stops in her tracks, closes her eyes, and tips
back her head. She takes a deep breath in. Yum! Mom is baking pies.
She throws her backpack on the couch and runs to the kitchen. "What are
you baking!?" "Hello to you, too!" Mom says with a laugh. Debbie gets close to
the 1960s, green, double oven with stove and squats down. "Can I see what it looks like?"
Mom has a sly look on her face. "Sure!" Debbie opens up the bottom oven. Nothing!
Where is it? I can smell it. But, I cannot see it. "Try the upper oven", says Mom
while lifting her up off of her feet. Mom pushes the oven light inside the oven.
"Oh, there it is! Momma, it looks delicious!" "I burnt the first one; it looked
quite dead." "What kind is it, Momma?" Mom set Debbie back down on
the floor, "I guess you will have to wait until you bite into it!"

Making Amends

Starla Criser

"This is my worst nightmare," Percy grumbled as he shuffled across the field. "All I said to Pickles was maybe she should exercise a little more."

His pal, Arnold, tottered nearby. "That doesn't sound all that bad."

Percy hadn't thought so, either. But the love of his life had gone all bristly in an instant. Her small brown eyes had gotten even smaller and pinned him with fury. Then she'd tossed his favorite pillow at him and told him to sleep outside.

He'd bristled himself until her eyes filled with tears, and she trembled. He'd felt lower than slime and left their home, knowing he needed to make amends. Which led him to this field with his friend.

He stopped to sit on his haunches and gaze around. "I just wanted her to go walking around with me. We go our separate ways too much."

"She thought you called her fat," Arnold said and looked around.

"I didn't say that," Percy protested. But he'd made her cry, so she must have interpreted what he'd said that way. He needed to get back on her good side. "Where the heck are they?"

Arnold sat up, too, and cocked his spiny porcupine head. "What exactly are we looking for? I forgot."

Percy sighed. Arnold was a good buddy, but his memory was a sad thing. He could leave his home to search for some tasty leaves or twigs and forget almost immediately where he was going. That's why they generally searched together.

"Pink flowers," Percy said, squinting into the sun and studying the field again.

"When did you start eating pink flowers?" Arnold asked in confusion.

Percy spotted a small batch of flowers across the field. "Not to eat, Arnie! For Pickles. Remember?"

Instead of waiting for his friend to respond, Percy scurried toward his goal. He saw purple flowers, yellow flowers, white flowers, and not one single pink flower. He really, really needed to find pink flowers. That was Pickles' favorite color.

Arnold strolled closer. "I remember now." He grinned, chuckling. "Pickles is mad at you."

Percy glowered. He ground his teeth in frustration, and his quills spread out, which only frustrated him more. There wasn't an enemy around. Clearly, he was his own worst enemy. He opened his mouth and said words that were misinterpreted.

Rather than discuss the problem anymore, he snagged a bunch of flowers, all colors, and take them home.

A few minutes later, he'd grabbed them and shuffled back across the field, the flowers gripped in his teeth. Arnold hadn't helped him but had strolled around, nibbling on this or that.

Catching up with his friend, Percy mumbled as best he could, "Okay, let's go back."

"Look what I found," Arnold announced with pride. He nodded to a big, fat pink flower next to him. "I'm going to take it home to my sweet Sally."

Percy hung his head in defeat. His friend had found what Percy had been searching for and didn't even know it. He'd already forgotten why Percy had come out to the field. His buddy was so happy about his treasure and pleasing his mate. No way would Percy ruin that for him.

He just hoped Pickles would like what he'd picked for her. Besides, he'd gotten her six flowers!

Should've, Would've, Could've

Don Boldea

I should've been born rich. I laughed so hard at the thought I got a stitch.

I would've become a philanthropist or an irreverent antagonist just for fun.

I could've become the POTUS or worked at the zoo bathing their only giant-sized hippopotamus.

Instead, I'm just a should've, would've, could've kind of guy. I'm the fellow who lies under an old oak tree, counting the marshmallow clouds floating through the sky. Ta-ta!

Big Thompson Canyon, Colorado

Bubbles

Don Boldea

I have an unusual goldfish named Odorous.

He is really fat and likes, now this is really strange, he likes to wear a chef's hat made of seaweed.

This crazy fish also likes to eat tomatoes. That's strange too, but that's okay. However, after he eats any portion of a tomato, he creates a steamy boil of bubbles in his eighteen by thirty-six-inch fish tank. It's like watching a skin diver's breathing apparatus suddenly being punctured.

When the bubbles surface a smell would be released, that would cause a flower bed of roses to wilt and totally corrupt a whole flowering nursery.

I have asked a number of ichthyologists if there is a zipper that exists that I could Gorilla glue to my goldfish Odorous and stop his unwanted fragrant explosions.

Doctor Ichthy said if there were such a zipper you could very possibly experience, without warning, the goldfish exploding. It's not a pleasant sight, smell, or clean-up. Plus, the aroma may last for some time in your bedroom, house, and neighborhood. I asked him, then what should I do?

He said, with a fissure wide smile, that I should give the goldfish to my most disliked relative, friend, or enemy and don't forget to tell them that the fish loves tomatoes.

Following Doctor Ichthy's advice, I gave my goldfish to my most odorous nephew, nicknamed Stinky. He was aptly named because one at a time all of his pets suspiciously disappeared only later to be found decaying in a shoe box under his bed.

This goldfish isn't going to disappear for a long, long time. That is as long as Stinky keeps feeding Odorous tomatoes and doesn't eat him for a snack. Rather, he eats him or puts him in a shoe box under his bed.... who would notice?

Catechism 101 with Sister Mary Walburga

Mary Denney

The new TV show Don't Make Me Laugh was filming in Wichita tonight. I had the first spot on the show. Three talent scouts would judge the contest. Of course, many more scouts would be watching. Since it was a talent show for comedians, I was excited to have made the cut. The audience would be fairly small and selected for their love of humor.

I had my costume and stage props ready. The costume was an official-looking nun's habit: a long black dress with a white Whipple and a black veil. My bedroom slippers made believable sandals. I'd wear a pair of old-fashioned gold rim glasses that looked like they were as thick as the bottoms of coke bottles. Better yet, they made my eyes look about three times bigger than they really are. Good for staring! I looked at myself in the full-length mirror. I looked like a penguin, with enormous eyes.

As curtain time approached, I was getting the usual anxiety feelings, known as "stage fright." I felt like my face was as bright red as a strawberry. And I was having a hard time not laughing that silly, giggly sound my mother said she recognized as a clue that I was doing something forbidden.

My props were a teacher's desk and chair, along with a ruler and a gallon plastic jug. I had a wastebasket too. I was planning to do a skit about a nun teaching a class in catechism for beginners.

As the curtain opened on my act, I was sitting at the teacher's desk and doing a roll call. The audience was my classroom. I stood up and came around in the desk's front and introduced myself. The glasses made me very dizzy and wobbly looking. That got a big laugh.

I looked the group over as if I was a drill sergeant inspecting the troops. I tried for an expression that looked like I found them very distasteful and unacceptable. That got another laugh. I was finally feeling a bit more confident.

I started off by saying, "Raise your hand if you want to go to Heaven." All hands went up.

Next, I said, "Raise your hand if you want to go today?" This time there were no hands raised.

I continued, "My job is to get you ready. However, it's up to you if you make it or not." Here, I stopped and looked them all over again, as if to indicate I didn't think they would make it. They laughed, and I was happy.

"Does everyone have a Bible?" As I perused the crowd, I spun around and grabbed the gallon jug. "Alright!" I raised my voice in disapproval. I grabbed my ruler and slammed it on the desktop. Blam! "You all need to spit your chewing gum into this jug."

I walked across the front row of the audience with the ruler in my hand. A few of the audience played along and acted like they were adding their gum to the jug. As I tried to put the jug down in the wastebasket, I missed it. I took a couple of stabs at it and finally picked up the basket and placed the jug inside. I got another big laugh.

"Now," I said, "The Bible is the history of man's encounter with his God. It is a lot like a history book, and it will be our textbook. It is divided into two parts, the Old Testament, and the New Testament. They are each divided into Chapters and will explain how God created the Universe and how He created us and how to get to Heaven. It is the glue that holds our path to Heaven together."

I had planted my cousin Bob in the audience, and he was to make some smart remarks from time to time. Sort of a heckler like you see at some events. After getting several more laughs, the show was over, and I had won the contest for the first week's show!

Dinner Party Gone Wrong
Coe Holden

I was having a yard party. My boss and his wife were there, along with the other guests. The steaks were almost done, the salad and baked beans were on the table, when the wind changed, and the temperature dropped about ten degrees.

I went to get my patio heater, and it was out of kerosene. My nosy neighbor was gawking over the fence and gave me his kerosene, and I thanked him for his charity, and soon all the guests were warmer and happy.

My neighbor's cat jumped over the fence, and my dog chased it. The cat and dog were running around the yard and knocked over the grill and the steaks. Hot coals went all over the yard and caught the grass on fire.

The cat jumped on the table with the dog in hot pursuit and knocked the salad and plates over and ran through the baked beans.

The cat ran between my boss's wife's legs and knocked her to the ground. She was wearing a short tight skirt and it came up over her waist.

Then we heard a loud clap of thunder, KerBoom, followed by a cloudburst.

We all ran for the house, and the wet, smelly dog followed. The rain put out the grass fire.

We stood there dripping wet. My boss said to his wife. "Let's go home!" And they and the rest of the guests left.

There I stood. looking at the mess and sat down and poured myself a stiff drink. The wet, stinky dog jumped in my lap. Anything that could go wrong went wrong.

The Pixie Did It
Coe Holden

I am a PIXIE. I am ornery.

You can't see me, but I am always here,
sometimes I like to play tricks on you.

When you can't find your glasses or car keys or anything else that
you have misplaced,
I let you look all over for them, and I keep moving them around,
and when you have given up, I put them back where you last had
them.

I also play with your mind as well,
like when you can't think of someone's name that you know,
or anything else, like a place you have been.

It is me who clouds your thoughts.

The next time you can't think of a word, a name, or where you misplaced
something—

Just say, IT MUST BE THE PIXIE DID IT.

The Carnival
Don Boldea

Now I ask you, who hasn't been to one of those traveling carnivals? Yes, if you are over sixty and live in a rural community, I bet you have.

I remember every time the carnival came to our town, I begged Mom and Dad to take me to see all of the attractions, especially the monkeys. Since I was unrelenting with my begging, they finally gave in and off we went.

It was about lunch time when we arrived at the gates. I love carnival food, so our first stop was the hot dog vendor. I ordered two of those luscious hot dogs, slathered in mustard and ketchup, a couple of generous spoons of dill relish, a modest amount of fresh white onions, and finally, a grand topping of shredded cheese. After all, I was barely a teenager and almost all teenagers have hearty appetites.

Dad loved to show off his target shooting mastery, and he always wanted to impress Mom and me. Of course, we had to stop at the shooting gallery. Painted tin ducks, bears, squirrels, and some funny looking little birds were the moving targets in front of a cheesy looking forest background.

Old eagle-eyed Dad would pick up a rifle and pull the trigger until the projectiles ran out. As usual, he won a prize. He was presented a fourteen-inch tall, dusty Kewpie doll. Dad's chest was so swollen nearly all the buttons popped of his shirt. Still, he presented Mom with the doll. Even when we got home later that evening his chest was still puffed up so much that we had to use a pair of scissors to cut off the reaming buttons, enabling him to take the shirt off.

After enjoying all the wonderful booths and amusement rides, we ventured down the promenade to the exotic animal exhibits. This was my favorite of all carnival presentations.

The first attraction was Tarzan the Ape Man's sidekick Cheetah! This Cheetah had to be the fifth or sixth generation Cheetah from the original. Yet the crowd was still entertained by the chimpanzee.

The bushy, you might even say shaggy, poorly kept chimpanzee was dressed in a tutu, wearing a tiara on its head. Cheetah then danced around the stage to some unrecognizable musical score from the end of a leash.

The chimpanzee looked embarrassed and very ashamed at the same time.

Even though letters were sent to appropriate authorities, that was the last time I begged to go to the traveling carnival.

Just a Bit of Fun

Starla Criser

Bert the buffalo snickered in amusement as he watched from a short distance away from the campground of the ranch hands from the Lazy Z. They were herding cattle down from the hills and herding a dozen greenhorns playing at being a cowboy.

It wasn't even dawn and already chaos reigned supreme. His friend Skinny Alfred, the cantankerous longhorn, was at his trouble-making best. He'd discovered everyone in the camp sleeping, except the trail guard. And the guard wandered off to take care of some personal business. A serious mistake, leaving the opportunity for Alfred to amble into camp. He took the shirking of duties as his chance to accept a personal dare.

His first ornery task had been to knock over the rope line, holding the reins of all the horses tied there. Thrilled at the unexpected freedom, the mounts were now racing through the cattle herd rounded up yesterday. The pounding hooves of both horses and cattle had awakened the stunned, half-asleep greenhorns, and the thoroughly annoyed hands scrambling to catch the horses. The amount of colorful swearing would burn most people's ears.

Bert snickered again. With all the cowboys running around like wild men, Alfred went on to more playful work in the campground. He tromped through the main campfire, sending logs and whatnot flying all over the place.

He strolled toward the cook's old-fashioned covered wagon and lowered his head. Using his enormous horns, he knocked the wagon off-kilter. Pots and pans and lots of other stuff clanged around, making all kinds of noise.

It drew more attention from the confused tenderfoots, keeping their distance from the "crazed" longhorn. One of the surprised greenhorns had come out of his tent, holding a small container, and spooning out a glob of something whitish before dropping it all at his feet. Yogurt, Bert believed. He'd seen people eating it before, although he did not know why. Sometimes they scrunched up their faces when they ate it.

Anyway, good old Alfred sure could create havoc.

Bert decided it was his turn to have a bit of fun. He ambled toward Cowboy Tom's, the supposed "man in charge," abandoned tent. Bending down, he eased inside, smashing into a cot and turning it onto its side. He nosed around until he spotted a crate holding some curious objects. Notes paperclipped together. A small phone thing he'd seen some men using occasionally. Other boring stuff.

He backed out of the tent and found a couple of cowboys heading his way. They didn't look happy. It appeared Alfred had disappeared, and these fellows seemed to think he'd caused this mess. He shot them a glare that slowed them down long enough for him to make his escape. They didn't come after him. Even if he was sort of the "ranch pet," few men would take on a buffalo scowling at them.

When I Say I Love You
Don Boldea

When I say I love you, it's like Frank Sinatra singing "Do-b-do-b-do." It's like caressing a savory, super-loaded Great Plains pizza. Oh, Greta, I love you.

Every day at lunch, I jump up from my desk, put on my pandemic mask, and rush down and visit the always on-time food truck. No hamburger will do, it tastes too much like a soccer shoe. No, I need his specialty, something that reminds me of you. I've got it!

I need a soft, silky kneaded dough rolled thin with a spread of smooth garden tomato sauce infused with sweet basil, rosemary, thyme, garlic, and parsley. I need a spicy covering of Italian pepperoni and sausage. I need a fine layer of thin bias-cut red, green, and yellow sweet peppers.

Next, I need rings of tasty white Vidalia onions spread about with a layer of sliced button mushrooms. I also need a smattering of diced red Mexican chili peppers. Oh yes! Finally, it must be topped off with a caressing and smothering mound of macaroni and cheese.

The pizza must be stone-fired, so all ingredients and dough are married into a full kiss of loveliness, texture, and taste. That's a Great Plains pizza.

As I'm eating the Great Plains slice of pizza, I think of you while dancing the flamingo down the street. There is no need for music or stopping at red traffic lights.

When I say I love you, being with you simply makes me as happy as a Great Plains pizza.

Oh, Greta, I love you!

R. Tobey

My Birth

Don Boldea

I've been six months in my mother's belly (by the way, this is a G-rated story). I'm bored. In another three months floating in this water balloon, I will be severely wrinkled and bored out of my mind. However, it is kind of fun floating around in this somewhat cramped space.

I'm curious: will I be an adorable baby or a long-haired hippie-looking Musk Ox? You know the kind, like an eight-hundred-pound hairball.

My dad was a good-looking fellow, and my fraternal grandfather and grandmother were a gorgeous-looking pair. My mother was gorgeous, but my maternal grandfather and grandmother, well, they were okay. So, what will I look like?

Hey, out there! It's a little cramped in here! How about a little kick in the bladder, will that help let you know I'm ready to come out? How about some pressure on all parts of your body's innards? How does that feel. Gotta go to the bathroom?

Good, here comes the doctor. I ask you now, how can a person with just one long eyebrow instill confidence in his doctoring skills? Go figure. Anyway, he says, "It's time for your child's birth. All the planets are aligned." What the heck does that mean? Then he loudly asks, "Ready? Thumbs up, that's an A-Okay in my books."

There's my poor mother, in a chair-like thing elevated at a 45-degree position with her feet in those things called stirrups, five miles apart.

And me, I'm not certain if I'm up or down. Since this is my first time, I'm absolutely not sure what's next. Oh-oh! What was that whooshing water sound?

Let me tell you what happens next. I hear someone say, "Push!"

Have you ever felt like you've been dropped into a very large black hole and expected to come out alive? What's worse is a cord (they call an umbilical something or other) keeps trying to pull me back to where I want to escape from. I've made it through that stage, well almost.

Next, I hear, "There's the head. Get ready, push!" I was blown out into the world like a photon torpedo fired from an interstellar star ship. I flew through the air and through the hands of both the doctor and his nurse assistant.

I soared across the room at light speed, sliding across the cold tile floor, bouncing off the opposite wall, rebounding like a yoyo, the umbilical effect again. I finally landed in the doctor's hands. He must have been a fan of astronauts returning from space because he joyfully yelled, "Touchdown!"

After all of that, he had the audacity to hold me upside down and slap my butt. I didn't know I was supposed to cry, so I didn't. Well, that pervert slapped me again.

If my arms had been long enough, I would have slapped the doctor's face, skunked him, and made a baby-like cooing sound with a twinkle in my eye.

This traumatic birth experience could have had a devastating effect on any typical human being's psyche. But noooo, it only made me a unique individual.

I am now married, have two children, and my wife's family has adopted me as part of their family. They visit us here on Earth every other year and then we visit her family every other year on their planet. Think about it.

My parents tell our Earth family that my family and I are on a secret research assignment in a far-off land to cover for our lengthy time from the family.

Now, telling the true story of my birth may seem to have been a bit outrageous. However, you must admit that many of the physical references are true and correct.

But, I must also remind you of what the comedian Lily Tomlin's Edith Ann character would say, "And that's the truth . . . thuuuuuuupppppppps!"

The Dare

Phil Lonas

My sister was going to have some leftover spaghetti and meatballs for lunch. My brother dared me to put some worms in the pasta and hide them in the sauce. And so, I did.

I dared him to squish a cricket in one of the meatballs. And so, he did.

My sister twirled her fork in the pasta and took a big mouthful, worms, and all. She took one bite and spit it out in her napkin.

My brother and I laughed.

She said, "Mom, why does this taste so slimy?"

My brother nudged me and said, "Let's not bug her with the details." Then he cracked up over his own excruciating wit.

Giving It Her Best
Starla Criser

The annual secret late-night Andersonville Zoo Talent Contest was finally happening. Everyone had practiced so hard for it. Then a change in zoo staff in their schedules had worried the animals. Could they still do it?

Penny shoved those thoughts aside. Their plans had all worked out. The sneaky chimps who always managed to get out of their area whenever they pleased had done their assigned task. They prepared special water laced with a small sedative and distributed it to the night staff's breakrooms. When the staff woke up, the contest would be over, and the animals would all be safely back in their designated zoo homes.

Penny was so excited that she could barely stay still. She was giggly. This was such an important night for her, for everyone around her.

In the dimly lit backstage area of the zoo's amphitheater for special concerts, she glanced around at the other talent show contestants waiting nearby. Zinnia, the hippo's sides trembled with impatience. Tony the rabbit's nose twitched with nerves. Ginger, the fainting goat, struggled to keep her eyes open and mumbled, "Don't fall down. Don't fall down."

Beyond their area, she heard the audience of zoo animals clapping and cheering on Betty, the giraffe, tap dancing on the stage. Penny was proud of her for doing it when her peer giraffes didn't think she could do it.

Penny firmly believed you could do whatever you wanted to do, and she wasn't worried about her act. She had this! She'd practiced a hundred times. No, a thousand times. No one would expect a ballerina penguin doing a pirouette, not even a sort of odd one like she did.

Something distracted her from watching Betty. She sniffed, sniffed deeper, and heard Harold the camel groaning in embarrassment. Nerves had finally gotten to him, and he'd had an "accident" that was stinking up the small area. Poor guy.

Everyone tried to move away from the big, brown blob while Betty danced off the far side of the stage. Then the announcer called out, "Alfred is next on the program."

Alfred, the massive, gentle polar bear standing next to Penny, jumped nearly a foot on hearing his name. Then her best zoo friend stood frozen in place, barely breathing. Panicked.

The announcer called his name again, and Penny could tell the audience was frustrated with his lack of appearance.

She waddled closer to him in her glue_d-on strawberry slippers. She touched his huge arm, and he looked at her, fear in his eyes. Fear was so strong she could almost taste it. In a second, she knew he would turn and flee.

"You can do it, Alfred," Penny said with faith in her friend. "I know you can." She gave his furry back a slight nudge.

He drew in a deep breath, steadied himself, and strolled out. He towered over the much shorter announcer, who stepped quickly away, though he looked like he wanted to run.

Alfred gave a brief glance toward Penny for reassurance.

She gave him her best encouraging smile.

After another awkward few seconds, he began singing in his deep, bass voice. "Tale as old as time. True as it can be. Barely even friends."

He hesitated in his lines from the "Beauty and the Beast" song. He looked at Penny once more.

She flashed him another smile and waved a flipper at him to go on singing.

He faced the fascinated audience again. "Then somebody bends. Unexpectedly Just a little change. Small, to say the least." He pulled in a breath. "Both a little scared. Neither one prepared. Beauty and the Beast. Ever just the same."

By the time he finished the song, there wasn't a dry eye in the place. Not in the audience. Not backstage with the other contestants. And Penny was sobbing her heart out at his powerful performance.

Finished with his song, Alfred moseyed off the stage. He held his head high, and pride glistened in his eyes. He stopped in front of Penny, rumbling, "That was for you, my little friend. You gave me the courage to come here today. You believed in me."

She sniffed back another sob at his heartfelt words. "Yes, yes, I did."

"And next is our surprise ballet performance by Penny."

Penny's heart pounded in her chest, and her eyes widened. She couldn't seem to move.

When Alfred put his massive paw on her back, he smiled and walked with her to center stage.

The announcer gaped at them. "Are you... Are you both...?"

Alfred's roar of a laugh sent the announcer scurrying away and had the audience gasping. Until he turned, stepping a few feet away from Penny. He gave an impressive bow, saying, "Show them what you can do, my friend. Make everyone see that anyone can do what they believe they can."

He bowed once more and left the stage.

Penny took his words to heart and let the music to Swan Lake played on a stereo behind her fill her soul. This ballet had long been regarded as one of the most demanding ballets. But she could do this! She was sure that no one anywhere would ever perform it with such grace and skill. Okay, being a penguin, she couldn't do the leaps as high as a human dancer. But it didn't matter to her, and the audience didn't care about that either. They applauded enthusiastically throughout her entire five-minute performance.

When she stopped in the middle of the stage, breathless from exertion, she started to collapse. In a flash, Alfred was there for her. He scooped her into his muscled arms and held her up to face the still clapping audience.

Penny had been the last performer. After some quick deliberation by the judges just off the stage, they would soon announce the winner. The other contestants stepped out and surrounded Alfred and Penny. Everyone waited anxiously for the decision.

Alfred glanced at the others around them, getting subtle nods, and moved to the front of the stage. He looked intently down at the judges. Then up at the audience.

Penny wiggled in his arms, whispering, "Put me down. This is embarrassing."

He did, but he put his hand on her head to keep her standing in front of him. Again, he looked from the silent judges to the expectant audience. "All the performances tonight were good." He smiled down at Penny. "But Penny's was by far the best. I proclaim her the winner."

"You can't—" Penny protested, touched by his pronouncement.

"I did."

The wild applause from in front of her and behind her had Penny blinking back tears of happiness. She'd done it! She'd actually done it! But how could she top this performance next year?

Writer's Block

Coe Holden

Writer's Block, I look at the clock,
It's 2:30 AM and not a single word on the paper.
Been at it all evening and not a thought or a clue for my labor.
My mind is dead, nothing in my head,
I think I will just go to bed.
I feel I am as dumb as a rock,
It must be Writer's Block.

Writer's Block
Bonnie Lacey Krenning

As I sit here in my chair and rock,
I'm thinking about my Writer's Block.
They say it's just a crock of you know what.
Not so, I'm weary of my Writer's Block.
Believe me, it's not a crock of you know what.

Writer's Block
Phil Lonas

Here I sit broken hearted,
try to write but can't get started.

I put pen to paper and try to think,
but all my ideas just seem to stink.

History, mystery, poetry, and crime.
great topics but none of them mine.

So how shall I cope this indecision,
I'll just say heck with it all and go watch television.

INSPIRATIONAL

Dust If You Must

Rose Milligan

Dust if you must, but wouldn't it be better
To paint a picture, or write a letter,
Bake a cake, or plant a seed;
Ponder the difference between want and need?

Dust if you must, but there's not much time,
With rivers to swim, and mountains to climb;
Music to hear, and books to read;
Friends to cherish, and life to lead.

Dust if you must, but the world's out there
With the sun in your eyes, and the wind in your hair;
A flutter of snow, a shower of rain,
This day will not come around again.

Dust if you must, but bear in mind,
Old age will come and it's not kind.
And when you go (and go you must)
You, yourself, will make more dust.

The Last Dance

E.L. Morrow

I wasn't spying on her. Well, of course not. I didn't know there was anyone in the house. I thought I was alone in the attic of an abandoned house. But there she was—dancing. Her dance was mesmerizing. In the dim morning light, I could not determine her age. She seemed young, but her dancing was mature.

I felt like an intruder. I witnessed something that should be private, but I couldn't turn away. Her movements were fluid and un-selfconscious. What's the saying? "Dance like no one is watching." Well, she danced for the pleasure of the dance. I wished I had understood more about ballet. The dance appeared to be a complete performance from—what is it called?—muscle memory, that's the term.

The dance was so captivating that I barely noticed her strange apparel. She wore western boots, and her tutu was much too long— perhaps a repurposed crinoline from the 1050s—my sister had some when she was a pre-teen.

It hit me; the dancer believes she's alone. I'm trespassing. When I arrived during the night, the place appeared deserted. No signs of habitation; no lights or heat. Now that I think of it, there was no dusty odor, either. And the sleeping bags I found in this attic were not old or musty.

Does she live here? Without heat or a phone in February? Something is strange here. I must be careful not to startle her.

How did I get into this situation? Guilt mostly; trying to make up for not being the father I wanted to be. My daughter called yesterday at 2:00 AM Eastern time. She's in some trouble and asked for my help. Her voice reminded me of the five-year-old who knew Daddy could fix anything. In reality, she is a fifty-two-year-old professional with grown children.

But she needed me. I would not refuse. Whatever it is, money alone will not fix it.

Thirty minutes later, I called her back with flight numbers and times: Baltimore, Chicago, Denver, rent a car, and drive three hours to her home. With luck, I'd be there by 8:00 PM Mountain time.

She mentioned a storm.

Luck was anything but good. Travel was filled with delays. It was 8:00 PM before I got on the ground in Denver. By the time I pulled away from the airport, I was facing six to eight hours of driving on snow-packed roads—if they stayed open to traffic. Our latest plan was I'd call my daughter in the morning. We couldn't predict how far I might get.

Less than an hour on the road, and all lanes came to a standstill. A pile-up two miles ahead promised to block the roadway for hours. Nothing to do but sit. Unless?

As a long hall trucker, I used to drive these roads. I was sure I remembered this part of the road. I'd simply travel around the roadblock.

Wrong again! I soon found myself on a farm road looking for a turnaround. The ground gave way as I was making a back-in turn. The vehicle's rear dropped into a ditch. Staying in the car was not an option. Too cold without the heater; death by carbon monoxide running the engine. The headlights revealed the shadow of a structure, perhaps a barn. It turned out to be this empty house, with three sleeping bags in the attic.

My reflections were interrupted as the dancer finished her routine, bowed to me, and handed me a laminated card. Printed in block letters, "I cannot speak. I CAN hear." Below, using a marker, she had written, "My grandson will return when the road clears … he will help with your car." Looking through the attic window, I saw the car, nearly covered by the drifting snow.

I expressed admiration for her dancing. "Your dance was beautiful; I didn't want to interrupt. I'm sorry to intrude. When I came in last night, I didn't know anyone was here. You see, my car got stuck …." She smiled, held up a hand, and wrote on the back of the card, "Thanks for being my audience. You need to leave now. Wait downstairs." She gestured toward the stairway.

I complied—still no cell signal.

Her grandson, Ralph, arrived about noon with a van and two helpers. I met him outside with apologies, and I started explaining. He replied, "I'm aware. It's not a problem. I need you to wait down here while we go up."

As he headed up the stairs, he turned and asked, "Did you see her dance?"

"Yes."

"Did she finish? Did she take a bow?"

Again, I said yes. He nodded, turned away, and continued up the stairs.

It shocked me when the two helpers carried her body covered with a sheet on a stretcher. Only then did I realize the van her grandson had driven bears a funeral home marking. I asked, "What happened? She was so vibrant. Had she been ill? When I saw her dancing, I thought she was a teenager."

Ralph told me, "The brain tumor had taken her speech. Before it took her movement, she wanted to dance in the home of her youth. Her doctor warned about an aneurysm rupture. She chose the risk, knowing she would have an audience. When I asked her how she could be sure, she said—well wrote, "Someone always gets stranded here during these storms."

R. Tobey

Grandma Sunshine

Sherry A. Phillips

(Sing loud and off-key)
"You are my sunshine, my only sunshine.
You make me happy when skies are gray.
You'll never know dear how much I love you.
Please don't take my sunshine away.

Grandbabies usually stop crying in fussy hours of late morning or mid-afternoon with this obnoxious abuse of sweet lullaby. My trick interrupts their whine of "I'm tired, hungry, too wet; help me, NOW!"

Grandma's off-key singing is a surprise. Like a "sucker hole" on a cloudy day A break in billowing overcast skies that let sun rays through giving pilots an escape from bouncy downdrafts to a less bumpy flight.

Startling song ruptures the needy mood of a cranky child flying them up to a sunshiny place. A place where a wet diaper is exchanged for dry, blanky found, and bottle ready. A place where Grandma's arms are warm, where her quiet voice reads, Ten Little Rabbits, and we dance off to dreamy sleep with a quiet lullaby.

(Soft singing)
"You are my sunshine, my only sunshine.
You make me happy when skies are gray..."

Keep on Trying
Coe Holden

Keep on Trying instead of Crying,

When you fall and you think that is all,

There is more to life.

So get up and smell the air and you know all is not fair,

And those who care will be there to help you through it all,

When you fall.

So instead of Crying just keep on Trying.

Love
Connie Holt

Time is on your side,
When it comes to being loved.
True love takes some time.

It's so very true;
To have a friend, be a friend-
Always uplift them.

When you least expect,
Someone will ask you to dance-
Perhaps forever!

Forgive your Loved ones.
Tomorrow is not promised,
Don't burden your heart.

Are you spurned in Love?
You can't make someone love you.
'Twas not meant to be.

Give parents a break!
After all, they lacked training,
Starting on Day One!

Your grandma asks you,
"Please do not text while driving"-
Show your love, obey!

Find a job you love,
And work can be so much fun,
You won't grow weary.

Cardinals thrill me!
I often spy them feeding.
God favors Sparrows!

Whisperer of birds
And sundry woods animals;
Listen in silence.

Forgiveness is good.
Without it, your stomach churns,
So let grudges go.

Narcissist stares,

Looking in your trustful eyes,

But does not see You!

Spend some time alone,

Listening to the birds sing

And watch the flowers preen.

*From Grandma's Haiku Passages for Youth by Connie Holt

R. Tobey

Kind Words

R. Tobey

Watch what you say
  and always be kind,
you never know the hurt
  you might leave behind.
We all have troubles
  and days that seem dark,
and problems to solve
  as time leaves its mark.
There's nothing worthwhile
  in speaking bad news,
but cheerful words
  are the best to choose.
Be sure that your thoughts
  encourage and uplift,
for building up another
  is a precious gift.

The Uninvited Dinner Guest

E. L. Morrow

Jewel Abbott was not easily angered, but the embarrassment she felt had to be laid at someone else's feet. This was not her fault.

The congregation her grandfather had helped start needed a new pastor. The search committee had previously interviewed three candidates, none of whom "turned out to be compatible." Mother Abbott, as she was fondly called by the younger members (well, mostly fondly), knew that the candidates had rejected them rather than the other way around. She suspected that meant they found the people here dull, overbearing, and basically banal.

The Interim Minister, who served the congregation for more than a year, had accepted another assignment, and would leave them in a month. That's why the dinner was so important.

The committee had a new prospective minister, and this one seemed to be the most promising of all. The chair finally had the good sense to turn to Jewel for help. She was told the committee wished to portray a degree of sophistication and elegance that seemed to be missing from their previous presentations.

"If it's elegance you want," she said, "then the Country Club is the place to be." She secured the private dining room for the final meeting and Dinner.

Everything went well for the tour of the city, potential housing locations, and church edifice. Things started going wrong when they arrived at the country club.

First, the manager, very apologetic, bowing and scarping, informed Mrs. Abbott that her party must wait in the lounge. The lounge was not a bad place. It is attractive, comfortably furnished, and pleasant. Ordinarily, people would be offered drinks there; however, this being a Pastoral Search Committee, she was unsure of the prospective pastor's view of drinking. The situation could become awkward.

More importantly, from Jewel Abbott's perspective, the

lounge is where the ordinary, common members of the club gather. While adequate, this was not the impression she wished to make. Most disturbing to Mrs. Abbott was the reason for the delay. The manager explained that a previous group had run over, and staff had just now gotten into the room to prepare it. The room must be properly cleaned.

After a twelve-minute and eighteen-second delay, which everyone would hear about at the next meeting of the Country Club Board, they were admitted to the room. Missing were two of the three fresh flower arrangements she had specifically requested. As soon as she observed the oversight, she began seething. However, before making a scene, she reasoned with herself, "no one else knows there were supposed to be three floral arrangements, so that can pass for now. But the manager will have some explaining to do."

The meeting was first. This was when Jewel realized that though the committee had been showing this couple around the afternoon, the one they were calling as pastor was the woman. The husband is a nurse, and with the wife is the minister, not the other way around as it always had been.

Well, she was still getting over this shock when it happened. Mrs. Jewel Abbott, a retired architect, Country Club recording secretary, Garden Club Founder, and past president of the DAR, observed a sight most horrible. There was a mouse in her private dining room.

The mouse was making its way slowly along the room's baseboard, looking for crumbs. It paused every few inches to nibble as if finding a bread crumb, a small piece of cheese, or perhaps a bit of meat from an appetizer tray. What should she do? Mrs. Abbott decided not to leave to summon the manager. Maybe no one else had noticed the intruder.

The guests seemed to give full attention to the conversation. A few spouses of committee members were a captive audience like herself to someone else's activity. The committee spoke of beginning dates, a return visit to meet the entire congregation before the vote, which was scheduled for four weeks from that Sunday. All this time, Jewel watched the mouse, which finally disappeared under the closet door. Now she could relax. No one had observed the mouse but her.

The food would arrive in a few minutes. David, the committee chair, asked the minister's spouse, the man, the nurse, to offer thanks for the food. He happily agreed and gave what seemed to Mrs. Abbott the longest prayer for a meal in the history of this Club. He asked for God's blessing on each person in the room, by name, all those who had shown them kindness at the airport, the hotel, even the cab driver. He went on to ask for comfort for the children who would go to bed hungry, protection for those traveling, and a special blessing for a particular leper colony in Zambia. Then, when she thought it could go on no longer, he ended by saying, "… and may our appetites be as appreciative as our little mouse companion."

To Mrs. Abbot's chagrin, half of those at the table stifled a giggle. Her humiliation was complete. But it was about to get worse.

The servers entered with trays stacked with prepared plates. The first in sat up a portable tray stand, placing his overloaded tray on it. All the food slid off the tray to the floor when the stand broke. Realizing what was happening, the waiter lunged to steady the stand. Too late to save any of the plates. To make matters worse, in the process, he caught the leg of his colleague's stand, tumbling all those plates to the floor as well.

Horror and apologies abounded. The waiter started to attend to the spilled food mess but was told in no uncertain terms to leave it. This time, Mrs. Abbott did leave the room. Her guests could hear her barking orders like a drill sergeant. Those in the room sat quietly, suddenly interested in the wallpaper pattern or the detail of the flower arrangement on the table. More than a few were glad that the anger they were witnessing from the hall was not being directed at them.

In minutes, they replaced the meal. The wait staff carried each plate individually and offered an apology as they placed a plate before each diner. The manager personally served the last plate to the hostess. As the manager apologized, he asked, "is there anything else I can do?" He was told cover that mess.

The pile of broken plates, dented lids, and food was covered by an oversized white tablecloth.

Everyone seemed unsure how to continue. The eating began. The prospective pastor spoke up, "At the moment, this may feel awkward and embarrassing. I'm sure that in the days ahead, we will look back on this evening with fond memories. Please understand that these unfortunate events will not affect our decision." Everyone breathed a little easier.

Jewel thought, "Back on track. Finally." As everyone continued eating, the quiet returned, as did the mouse. Continuing its journey around the baseboard, it came upon a white tablecloth, slipped under it, and let out a squeal of joy that summoned five more mice. As long as it lasted, those mice were in heaven.

Ultimately, none of this mattered. The pastor received and accepted the call. She faithfully served the congregation for several years. When leaving, they asked her what had caused her to come here. She said, "That wonderful dinner at the country club. Everything went wrong. But everyone kept their cool. I thought if they can adjust to problems that well, I want to work with them."

Old Age Is Upon Us
Coe Holden

Old age is upon us, our youth is left behind.

Now life will start to unwind and by and by it will be time to say,

It has been a good time.

Good times are many, bad times are few.

We look at life with a good point of view.

When times are bad, and you think you are at the end of your rope,

Count your blessings because there is always hope.

The Coming
Coe Holden

While talking to a pastor about the hereafter and what is on the other side,

He tells me of a great place where there is no want or suffering any more.

He said the end may be near, but we don't know when.

So, make peace with yourself and ask for forgiveness,

for the judgment day is coming.

Be ready because it could come without warning,

It could be at night or in the morning.

End of the Rainbow

Coe Holden

When I leave this earth,

I'll not be far from you.

I'll be like a faint light in the dark,

Or a fleeting shadow or a slight breeze on your cheek
.

I'll wait for you on that great cloud in the sky.

And when you join me,

We will go and find the streets paved with gold

At the end of the rainbow.

MEMORIES

Dancing in the Kitchen

Nancy Breth

For Mom (Betty Miller 5/13/25 – 1/4/18)

My daughter Carrie, son-in-law Vince, and granddaughter Kayla greeted Mom and I with "Merry Christmases" and warm hugs. Our annual Christmas celebration (Christmas 2013) at their home was about to begin. But this year, Mom and I both were struggling to be merry.

A long, hard year for all the family was ending. But only the beginning of the increasingly rapid decline in Mom's physical and mental health. The diagnosis of Lewy body dementia earlier in the year was particularly devastating. Our hearts were breaking watching time take away more and more of the mother and the grandmother we all once knew.

The most difficult part for me was her constant complaining about her plight in life. Mom had never been one to always look on the bright side of life; but now at 88 going on 108, she seemed determined to live the rest of her life in the state of Misery and to make us all feel guilty because we didn't want to move there too.

I had been trying so hard to be loving and understanding and patient with Mom after picking her up at her apartment. I patiently walked alongside her out of her apartment, held the car door while she got in, put her walker in the back seat, then buckled her in and started up the car.

"Where did you put my sunglasses? You forgot! I knew you would, you always do! You know I have to have those! Here's my key. Go back and get them."

"Yes Mom, sorry I forgot." I sighed as I pulled the car into a parking slot so I could run in and get her sunglasses.

Back in her apartment I reviewed the list of things I was supposed to help her remember whenever she was going out: Her pills, a snack in case the meal is not ready at exactly noon or 5:00 p.m., her list of medications and allergies in case we must go to the emergency room. I came close to snitching a Xanax (for her anxiety and panic attacks) from her prescription bottle; but knew she counted them every other day.

"Look out for that lady who is backing out over there!" Mom screamed as she braced herself for a crash when I started up the car again; but still had the car in Park.

She panicked and braced herself at only two of the three stoplights on the way there and only three times inhaled sharply, held her breath, and closed her eyes as if praying as I hit potholes and bumps along the way.

By the time we walked in the door, I was feeling 88 going on 108; but after hugs from Carrie and Vince and granddaughter Kayla; well, who cannot feel merrier after a hug (except my mother, of course).

Once we got there, Mom kept the complaints to a minimum. And I managed to work myself up and out of the doldrums that had snatched the "Merry" right out of me on the drive there.

It's not that I minded being the dutiful daughter (along with her other two dutiful daughters)—spending the day with her at least once a week, taking her to all of her doctor's appointments, doing her laundry and grocery shopping, coming over whenever her "little people" (Lewy body dementia hallucinations) were getting out of hand or when she had a bad stomachache and thought she needed to call an ambulance when she was constipated. It was the ungratefulness and her attitude of my never being able to please her—never being a good enough dutiful daughter.

All I wanted this Christmas was for Mom to be happy for just a little while. Or just pretend to be enjoying herself. Was that too much to hope for?

I was having a great time visiting with Kayla and Carrie and Mom while Vince, our gourmet chef, was preparing our Christmas feast. But when Mom started telling her "Poor-me" story about how I forgot her sunglasses again and hit every bump along the way there, I felt my heart grow heavy with gloom.

The next time Mom had to go to the bathroom, instead of dutiful daughter jumping right up to help her, I let Vince help her up the step from the family room into the kitchen on the path to the bathroom.

The television was tuned to a station playing Christmas songs and had just started playing I'm Dreaming of a White Christmas. After making it up the step with her "knees that are about to give out on me," Vince pulled her into a waltzing position and asked her to dance.

I couldn't believe my eyes—my mother was smiling! And not just a teeny lift at the corners of her mouth. That perpetual frown had transformed into a face filled with a warm glowing light that filled the entire house as she and Vince waltzed in circles across the kitchen floor. This starry-eyed stranger looked like a schoolgirl at her first dance, not my mother. Not the mother who had slowly, sadly become someone for me to take care of instead of the strong, life-loving woman who once enjoyed taking care of me and all her loved ones.

Through tear-filled eyes, I watched as Vince helped Mom glide gracefully across the floor, forgetting her throbbing knees and the stomach pains that were her constant companions. She seemed to be dreaming of "White Christmases" in her past or doing the two-step to The Tennessee Waltz (their favorite song) with Dad at their 40th wedding anniversary. The glow on her face reflected the joys that had been hidden underneath her pains.

Her radiant smile took me with her, remembering the Christmases she made merry for her five children and then all the grandchildren, too. She would make everything in our feasts from scratch! The candy, the cookies, the cinnamon rolls, the homemade bread with hand-churned butter. The laughter and the joy we all shared every time our family would get together at Mom and Dad's for the holiday celebrations. Mom would spend hours and hours lovingly preparing the feasts and making and shopping for special gifts for all at Christmas. While all those years we kids, and the grandkids so often took for granted all the long hours that went into her loving preparation for holiday gatherings.

Lost in the music, she forgot about her fading eyesight, the tremors that made it difficult to sign her name on the Christmas cards she sent out each and every year with help from her daughters.

Forgot for a moment the strangers (hallucinations) that kept invading her apartment and making her fearful in a place where she once felt safe and secure. Forgot that her future would be an ever-increasing dependency on her daughters who had lives of their own. And how she hated depending on them for all those simple little things that had become so difficult for her to do now.

Gliding in the arms of her grandson Vince, she let herself go back to who she once was and always will be at heart—a young woman ready to take on the world, a woman in love with life. A strong, vital woman whose only true desire in life and genuine joy was to take care of her husband and her children and then her grandchildren, too.

I got my Christmas wish—Mom was happy for a while. And I got so much more.

I got a glimpse inside that great big heart of Mom's. That place where she holds this deep and forever love for me, for all her family. A love she once knew so well how to express when everything was working right (her mind and her body). The home-cooked meals and hand packed school lunches. The brand-new handmade clothes she made for all five of us kids all pressed and hung in the closet at the start of each school year. Watching over us to make sure we didn't kill each other when we were playing games outside. Staying up most of the night making my wedding gown, and there for me to take care of me and my babies when we were going through the divorce. Her career was taking care of Dad, me and my two brothers and two sisters. A thankless job where we all took her great love and sacrifice of self for granted. I understood her joy at being treated like a vital woman instead of a dutiful obligation.

It reminded me she was still there—that starry-eyed little girl, that woman in love with life, that mother and grandmother who loved taking care of us. Remembered that I just had to keep reminding her of the life-loving woman she was, as my dear son-in-love Vince did so well that day. She may have forgotten how to cook a Lean Cuisine dinner in the microwave or how to balance her checking account; and not hear well enough to carry on a conversation without us all raising our voices. But she still remembered how to dance—letting the music in her heart lead the way and dare her tired old body to keep up.

***

Mom passed peacefully into God's arms after a stroke at 91.

She lived a full, rich life, until the final years. Those last few years were not kind—to her or us loved ones. It became more and more difficult to remember that vital, life-loving woman she once was. More of a struggle to remember she wasn't intentionally being ungrateful for my help. Increasingly sad to know and understand the pain she was going through that nothing, no one could take away.

But now, after time has had its way with the heavy grief of those final years and of her passing, I can let go of the pain and remember the mom I saw dancing in the kitchen. Remember her glowing with pride for the celebrations of life she made happen for this great big happy family she and Dad gave their hearts and souls and whole life's work to. I have forgiven and let go of the moments she couldn't see through her pain. And will remember Mom two-stepping with Dad to The Tennessee Waltz at their 40th wedding anniversary. And all the beautiful memories she and Dad had made happen in my life.

And now I am so grateful she is happy every moment while she is Waltzing Across Heaven with the Love of her Life. Thank you, Mom, for everything!

My Goose Was Cooked
Mary Denney

I didn't get A+s in Home Economics without being an exceptional cook. My home economics teacher, Mrs. Houston, with her fastidious and demanding expectations, turned out some very accomplished success stories. There were only nine of us in our class and we could all cook and sew to her very high specifications. Presentation was the hallmark of her students. If it looked good, it tasted better.

Each semester, we were required to hand in all our recipe cards for inspection. She wrote our semester grade on the top, right-hand corner of the top card. A brief note usually followed my A+, such as "One who knows how and does good work!"

I've had two husbands, and both declared that I was the best cook they had ever known. My oldest son became a chef of some renown in Chicago, Illinois. My oldest daughter has also competed with chefs from France, Italy, and China. Both attribute their skills to their mother.

A meal going horribly wrong just didn't seem to be in the cards for me. I had watched all the TV chefs from Julia Child to Graham Kerr, "The Galloping Gourmet." I had cooked three meals a day for my family 364 days a year and just didn't know how to do it wrong.

That was until my husband shot a goose. His parents had a farm in the heart of the Flint Hills, and we were there almost every weekend. His father was a wonderful gardener and produced enough vegetables for me to put up for the winter, either by canning or freezing and milk and eggs for our little family the year around. We also had fish from the ponds on the farm and ducks, quail, and prairie chicken. Of course, I prepared them all with great success.

As we were driving home from the farm one Sunday evening, my husband slammed on the brakes and drew my attention to a gaggle of geese on the large pond west of the farm. Those not in the water looked like black and white pigs. They were as big. My husband grabbed his shotgun from the back of the car, and as I had on sandals, and could not walk through the pasture to get to the pond, I stayed in the car. He followed the fence line along the east side of the pond and went past it to the south before circling around the pond dam and sneaking up to the top of it, where he could get a good shot. He field-cleaned it and we took it home.

I called Mrs. Houston and told her of my challenge, and she said, "Whatever you do, don't cover the roaster. It will cook in the wild flavor." She suggested I stuff the cavity with a quartered onion, a couple of stalks of celery, an apple, and lay strips of bacon on the breast. It sure sounded good to me. I didn't have an apple but thought I could substitute an orange.

It was a good thing my roaster was deep, as that goose cooked and produced so much grease you could have oiled every hinge in the house and lubricated several cars. I ended up burying the whole mess, as the meat was horrible to taste. To make matters worse, I stubbed my little toe carrying the darn thing out to the backyard. My husband nicknamed me, "Stubby."

A field of hay bales in the hills near Weston, Missouri.

Growing Up
Sherry A. Phillips

Halfway up the block to 1515 on North Poplar is the house where I grew up. Built before World War II, green and white asbestos shingles cover the frame around two bedrooms, one bath, corridor kitchen with a dining and living room combined. It had a full basement.

Through the kitchen screen door, I see peach trees by the back fence, the barrel where we burn trash, an old Elm tree to shade us when we play canasta on a folding table just a leash-length away from where we tether Spotty, our black and white cocker spaniel. The big garden is behind the garage just past the clothesline.

Mom and Dad have the front bedroom. Sister, Sheryl, and I share the back bedroom with water cooler in the window. A double bed in the corner of the basement sitting on an old living room rug is the guest room when our half-brother, Bill, or half-sister, Barbara, stays on the weekend. They live with our grandparents. We don't have the same dad.

Every morning Mother stands at the stove stirring Cream of wheat. Dad shaves and takes a hot bath leaving the medicine chest mirror steamed over when Sheryl and I have to brush our teeth. Dad's Old Spice aftershave smell hangs heavy in the moist air.

Mother bakes fresh peach pies and sends us out on the front porch with lemonade. In July, we bring quart mason jars up from the basement to sterilize. Tomatoes are ready to can.

The year I turned 16 Dad left us and sued Mom for divorce. A "for sale" sign was staked in the front yard in front of the Mock Orange bush. Mom and Sheryl and I packed up the good memories and moved into a basement apartment on South Hydraulic leaving my childhood behind.

Take My Hand

E. L. Morrow

One can learn much about a person by looking at their hands. My mother's hands were shapely, with longish fingers. In her youth, she played the piano and violin. For a while, she taught piano. She was skilled with a sewing machine, or needlework, due in part to her hands.

On the other hand, my father's fingers were stubby and more muscled. His work on the farm in his youth and later as an auto mechanic, carpenter, roofer, and HVAC installer added visible scars from cuts, burns, and scratches. His rough and callused hands told the story of how hard he had worked to support his family.

Hands are not only for work but can create, protect, or even injure. The hand can also elicit or express emotion or communicate as through sign language. Another way we use our hands is to hold the hand of another.

There are at least four kinds of holding hands. A parent or other adult figure reaches out for the child's hand while crossing a street or in a crowded place. Holding hands takes nothing from the child's accomplishment of being out in the big world—navigating on their own. For the parent, there is extra security, like nothing bad can happen to my child while I hold their hand.

I'm sure as a child that I held a parent's hand, but those specific memories elude me. I remember as big brother taking my younger sister's hand as we walked to school when she was in first grade, and I was in the sixth. Though we still walked together to and from school, she no longer wanted my hand about halfway through that year—a show of her independence.

Similarly, as a parent, my young children took my hand as we walked the neighborhood, in the mall, at the park, or when going to a doctor's appointment. At first, I reached for their hand; later, they would reach up to mine; finally, they didn't want my hand because,

"I'm a big boy/girl now, Daddy." All too soon, the day came when they didn't want me in the same county because I might embarrass them.

A different type is the tentative handholding of young lovers. I remember the girls with whom I would like to have held hands or talked or asked on a date, but without a car, money, and few social graces, those activities played out only in my head. While double dating during college, I remember tentatively reaching out to hold my date's hand. It seemed like something I was supposed to do. But the reality could never live up to the hype holding hands had been given by my more sophisticated friends. For me, it was a letdown. But like most things in life, I discovered the more I practiced, the better it felt and the more meaning it took on.

Now, in the later years of life, I experience a third—more mature practice of hand holding. When my life mate of nearly thirty-five years takes my hand, or I hers, while watching TV, or a movie, fixing a meal together, driving down the street, or falling asleep—I am reminded of the many that have gone before. The afternoon she was in anaphylactic shock as I prayed the Benadryl would take effect quickly. Or the touch when she bandaged my bleeding head so we could get to the emergency room. Also, the many times she massaged my aching back or feet.

Now days when our hands touch, it no longer brings the electricity or fireworks it once did, but the memory of those hours of joy and excitement lingers. Now the touching of hands communicates love and tenderness. The hands remember even what the brain has forgotten, or the tongue forgets to say. Touch for love; touch for health; hold the hand that holds your heart.

There is a fourth, a sacred holding of hands. These occasions come to pastors, nurses, and some family members. Praying with another that their parent, child, or mate will recover from the accident, sickness, surgery, or illness of spirit. Taking another's hand as they make a profession of faith or unite with a particular community of ministry and service. Finally, most sacred of all, holding the hand of one as he or she departs this world.

May every handshake, pat on the back, or reaching for another reflect that sacred touch, compassionate caring, and restorative action. May peace and justice come to others through our hands.

R. Tobey

My First Baseball Glove

Phil Lonas

One day when I was twelve years old, my friends and I were playing a game of sandlot baseball. This was one of those days I was at my best. My hitting, fielding, throwing, everything was right on.

A coach named Redd was watching us. He always had the number one baseball team in the city, and they won the city championship every year. When we were finished playing, coach Redd called me over and said he wanted me on his team. I was so proud I thought my heart would jump right out of my chest.

When I got home, I was so excited I ran in and told my parents, "Coach Redd picked me to be on his team!" The problem was that I didn't have a baseball glove. Although money was tight, they knew how much this meant to me.

The next day my mom took me to Sears and Roebuck to buy my glove. There were two of them there. One for five dollars that even had the "Ted Williams" signature on it and another one for three dollars. I got the one for three dollars. I guess this was the best they could do. The only thing was this glove was flat. I mean flat. No matter how much saddle soap I put on it or how hard I tried to shape it, it just stayed flat.

Our first game was the next day. When I got there and pulled out my glove, everyone cracked up laughing. Even coach Redd. We ended up using it for second base. And that's the only action that glove ever saw, and I never pulled it out again.

Things were different back then. A lot of us kids didn't have baseball gloves. But we never had to play without one. When one team came in, and the other went out, the kids with gloves swapped out with the kids that didn't. I wonder if that type of sportsmanship still exists today.

We won the city championship that year. When I think back on it all, I remember how proud I was to be a part of it. And I laugh about using my glove for second base. And how fortunate I was to be as resilient as I was. It could have broken me. You know, years later, it even hurt a little when I threw that glove away.

Oklahoma
R. Tobey

Blessed Assurance

Sherry A. Phillips

"Mimi," Krystine cries
On a run into the church parlor
I kneel; receive her hug as
Slender arms
Encircle my neck
Small hands reach to pat my shoulders
Her quiet whisper in my ear,
"It'll be okay, Papa's in Heaven now"

Seven-year-old Derek lays a stick at each corner
To mark the length and width of the grave.
He points and asks his Daddy, "Is Papa's head up here or down
there?"
"If he's down in the grave, how can he be up in Heaven?"

"Can Papa see me?" Abby wonders out loud as she colors a picture
of flowers and
V-shaped bluebirds.

Long, dark weeks we weep,
Will the awful loneliness ever end?
The hole in our hearts heal?
Survival, is it possible?

"Babe," Roy would say to me,
You can worry,
Wonder,
Ask all the questions you want
But, as for me,
I'm content with the mysteries of God."

Baby Hannah was four months old eight years ago, but we have a picture of Papa holding her taken the day before he died. Ann Marie only 18 months now can point to his picture or his clock and say, "Papa!"

Written October 2010

My First Car?

Don Boldea

After my grandfather's passing and because I was loved above all the other twenty-three grandchildren and because I was the oldest grandson, I was presented the title to my grandfather's forty-eight, hard top and rusted maroon Plymouth sedan. I was fifteen and a half years old, and I was ready for a car of my own.

The Plymouth was a four door, flat head six and required a quart of bulk oil at the end of each day. The driver's floorboard was rusted out, kind of like Fred Flintstone's car. The front cloth seats were thread bare; the springs were showing and were a bit uncomfortable to sit on as you can imagine. The tire's tread had a couple of miles left before becoming completely bald and flat. Oh yes, the brake pads were basically worn off to the nubs and were now metal to metal squealing on contact with the drums.

One last thing, my grandfather had just overhauled the carburetor. When he had finished, he had a hand full of parts left over. Yet, the car still ran and ran well. He was a great carpenter, but a terrible mechanic.

I called her Rusty, and she could have been a lemon. Instead, even better than an old truck, she was as tough as a World War II Army halftrack.

Yes, my blue-haired grandma should have paid the ten dollars and had the car taken to the junkyard. But she wasn't born yesterday. She left her so loved and oldest grandson to figure out what to do with it.

I looked the gift horse over. I asked myself, what are you going to do with it? Where do you start? I finally developed a plan that didn't include junking it.

First things first, pay the tax, title, and tag obligation. Thank goodness there weren't any inspections required back then. And thank goodness the total fee was only eight dollars.

Next, clean the grease and gunk off the old six-cylinder engine. It looked like a brand new engine and actually sparkled in the moonlight, as if you were wearing sunglasses.

Mechanicals were the next items on the list. Replace the brake pads and turn the brake drums. Next, change the hydraulic cylinder boots and bleed the air from the system. Oh yea, buy four used tires with a bit more tread.

I cut an oversized piece of tin and bolted the piece over the open space in the driver's floorboard. I visited a salvage yard for some rubber mats to cover the floorboard repairs. That was easy and cheap.

I was just about finished. While at the salvage yard, I bought a couple bunches of cotton filler and tied them over and under the springs of front bench seats. For a couple more dollars, I also purchased a bench seat cover and installed it.

I'm now nearly to the end of my plan. I pulled the moon shaped hub caps from the wheels and shined them up with steel wool. I used beeswax to make them shine. Then I painted the wheels with Chinese red outdoor paint and reattached the hub caps.

Finally, I purchased two quarts of flat black wrought iron paint and a two-inch-wide brush. After lightly sanding the body, not the chrome accents, just polish them and then begin painting her from the roof downward towards the running board.

I admired this now beautiful machine. It was time to take her out for a test run. She flew down the street like a screaming eagle with its tail feathers a fire.

To show her off, I took Grandma for a ride. Returning home, I walked around and opened the door for her. Full of pride with my chest swollen, I asked, "What do you think?"

Without hesitation, she retorted, "I should have offered to sell you this museum classic." That made me awfully proud of my first car.

The Battle of Bear Trap Ranch

Donald Grabendike

It was a dark and stormy night in the country… Actually, it was a cold and starlit night in the mountains of Colorado, but I am getting ahead of my story.

In the fall of 1965, I was a student at Wichita State University in the school of business. Getting close to graduation meant more research papers and more time in the library where I met the girl that changed my life forever. Her name was Vicky, and she was a student librarian working on the second floor in the research department. While looking for a particular book, our paths crossed, and we got acquainted. Not being shy around girls, I asked her if she would like to go to dinner and take in a movie, to which she responded, "It sounds like fun."

Four or five dates later, she invited me to go on a ski trip with a youth group to which she belonged. With one small hitch, the bus was full, and I would have to drive my car. Not wanting to miss a trip to Colorado and the company of a cute girl, I promptly recruited two frat brothers to accompany me and help cover car expenses.

On December 26th, my younger brother Jim and Tom joined me in my beautiful red Chevrolet SS Impala to embark on a grand adventure to the Rocky Mountains. The following day, we drove to the Broadmore Ski Resort, where we spent the day gracefully gliding down the mountain, demonstrating our expertise on the slats. It was more like a crash and burn scene, as we were mostly beginners with only one previous ski trip. That night we returned to the Bare Trap Ranch, a long seven-mile drive up the Gold Camp Road and had supper in the dining hall.

Following dinner, we adjourned to the ice-skating pond, where I was in my world. For years I had spent the frozen days in Kansas, spinning and turning on the ice-skating ponds of Wichita. We had been skating for about half an hour when Vicky skated over to me and asked if I would help another girl who had never skated and was having a hard time. I responded with, "Sure, send her over."

Shortly after that, a short blond with shiny new white ice skates came wobbling across the pond for help. As she approached, I observed her performance and judged where to start with my instructions. With a smile, I said, "Sit down here. The first thing we want to do is to get your skates on tight."

After kneeling to tighten her laces, I looked up at her and politely said, "On second thought, the first thing we need to do is to get your skates on the right feet."

It was downhill from that day forward! Her name was Terry, she was an art major, and I was hooked!

The following day, Jim, Tom, and I went back to the ski slope to continue our attempts to conquer the mountain, or better expressed, as an experiment in self-destruction. We had a great day, and following dinner, we rushed to the skating pond to see the girls we had met the previous night.

To my disappointment, Terry, the little girl with her skates on wrong, could not receive further instruction. She had fallen while boarding the ski lift and was having trouble walking, with no possibility of further ice skating. As we set by the fire talking, I suggested I would take her on a tour of the Colorado Springs area since she could not go skiing. We went to the Garden of The Gods, the Cave of The Winds, and then took a short drive to Green Mountain Falls, which I had visited many times on family vacations.

On the fourth day, it was time to return home. Rather than traveling on the bus, Terry decided to ride back to Wichita in my red Chevy. When arriving at her home, being a polite young man, I carried her bags to the door where I was invited in to meet her parents.

When the moment arrived to introduce me to her parents, she said, "This is Don." With a giggle, she turned to me and asked, "What's your last name?" I have always wanted to know what her folks thought when their little girl came home with a boy, and she did not even know his last name. To hear Terry tell the story, she knew my name but just could not pronounce it.

Three months later, after seeing each other every day, we got engaged on April Fool's Day, and on August 20th we were married.

For a honeymoon, we went to the Colorado Springs area to visit the sites we had missed seven months earlier. While in Cripple Creek, we attended a melodrama, spent the night in the old Imperial Hotel, went down into a gold mine, and visited several abandoned mines; but the highlight was the Manitou Mountain Incline. We had a wonderful ride up, followed by a long walk up towards Pikes Peak.

Returning to the cable car, we were told that the lift was closed due to the fog, and we would have to walk down. This would not have been so bad, except it was getting dark. "No problem. I walked the trail two years ago, and I can find the way."

It wasn't long before I revealed my great navigational skills to my new bride. We were lost. I pointed to a string of lights in the distance to reassure Terry, telling her that those lights marked the path on which the cable car ran.

We worked our way to the lights, only to find that the path was too steep to walk down, so we sat down and scooted our way to the bottom of the mountain. It took ten minutes to go up the mountain, an hour and a half to get down, and a couple of holes in the rear of our new jeans.

The first few months indicated the many wonderful years to come. There were many great vacations, a hippie van, fast new cars, and old slow cars. The years have been incredible, and we would not have wanted to miss a single one.

After 30 years, Terry confided in me something that happened with her friend Marilyn that first night back in the girls' cabin. They tossed a coin to determine which one would go to lunch the following day with my friend Tom. Terry lost and got stuck with me.

Every war is but a series of battles and to the victor goes the spoils of war. Tom may have won the first battle, but I won the war 56 years ago.

Oh! My Toe!
Bonnie Lacey Krenning

There was an old log lying in the backyard. The bark had fallen off, so it was smooth. It was several feet long and really big around. I was six years old, and my little brothers and I liked to climb on it and run across it, trying not to fall off. The older brothers used it for a chopping block to split the wood for Mom's cookstove.

Late one afternoon, I saw my ten-year-old brother, James, chopping wood. I climbed up on the log and stood there, barefoot, watching him.

He yelled at me, "Git back in the house!"

I yelled back, "No, I don't have to!"

As I stood there, James continued chopping wood. Then, acting like the ax slipped, he chopped into the log, close to my feet, trying to scare me. It didn't work.

Trying again, he reached out toward my feet with the ax.

The ax stuck into the log. But it cut the end of my big toe at the back of my toenail, cutting through the bone.

I jerked my foot away. The end of my toe dropped over, hanging by a thin strip of skin and was bleeding.

I sat down on the log and started screaming at the top of my lungs. Daddy and two older brothers, who were plowing in the fields, heard the screaming and came running to see what was wrong.

When Daddy saw my toe, he pressed the end back in place and sent one of the boys to ask our neighbor, who had a pickup, to come over and take us to town to the doctor.

Daddy carried me inside to the kitchen, and Mom wiped the blood until my toe stopped bleeding.

Mom and Daddy relied a lot on folk medicine. The tradition was that Native Americans used tobacco as a pain reliever and healing medicine. Daddy just happened to have a chew of his home-grown tobacco in his mouth. He carefully pressed the tobacco on my toe and Mom wrapped it. Those were the days before antibiotics.

Our neighbor drove up in his pickup and took Daddy and me to town about ten miles away. The neighbor had called the doctor who was waiting in his office when we arrived. Daddy carried me in and sat me on the exam table. As the doctor unwrapped my toe, I could tell he was angry when he saw the tobacco there. I heard him quietly say "filthy," and saying other words I had never heard before.

He laid his instruments and needles and thread on the exam table beside me. Daddy watched as the doctor rinsed my toe carefully and picked the little pieces of tobacco from the wound with small tongs. Pressing the end of my toe back in place, he decided not to do stitches, and then he wrapped my toe in bandages.

The doctor told Daddy to unwrap my toe every morning and soak it in warm Epsom Salts solution for about an hour, then wrap it in clean, dry dressings and not to let my toe get wet, unless soaking it. In a couple of weeks, my toe had healed without being disfigured. And my toenail eventually grew back.

Mom and Daddy were convinced and relied on Epsom Salts for treating wounds after that. And I don't remember Daddy ever again using chewing tobacco on a sore or wound.

Oil well in a wheat field - Northern Oklahoma
R. Tobey

I Always Remember

Sherry A. Phillips

Spark plugs from an old dark green Buick soaking in gasoline in a flat-bottomed coffee can. That small is a reminder of good times helping my dad.

Dad saved an old toothbrush so I could scrub off the loosened grime. I learned dirty spark plugs make the engine run rough or could keep it from running at all. I didn't really care why they needed to be cleaned. I just enjoyed helping my dad.

When I think back to those days in the early 1950s, cleaning spark plugs was a pretty big job that Dad would let me help him do.

I liked it a lot better than ironing white starched cotton sheets for Mom on Tuesdays. It was even better than cleaning furniture with a dust rag soaked with lemon oil on Wednesdays or cooking peaches for pie picked from the tree out back by the fence where I used to climb and hide.

When my mind conjures up me as a little girl, my brain smells a perfume called "Evening in Paris" and the fragrance of white, orange blossoms on the bush by the front porch on a humid summer night. But when I pull up next to a gas pump, it is the odor of gasoline that reminds me of a coffee can, a toothbrush, and my dad.

International Family & Foods
Don Boldea

When I was born, little did I know I was joining an international family and their international festival of foods!

Let me start this delicious tale by introducing my father. He was the first generation born in the United States. His parents were from Hungary and Germany. Needless to say, growing up there was a lot of sour sauerkraut, bratwurst sausage and German beer.

My mother's family came from a collision of Germans and soft-spoken Southerners. The impact on traditional dishes always created a very unusual daily and holiday menu.

Mother was one of four brothers and two sisters. Her oldest brother Arnold was married to a beautiful Italian woman and boy, how I loved her homemade pasta dishes.

Uncle Loren was married to a Latino. She was able to create the most delectable spread. Hot, spicy, and one just on the milder side of fire kept me at the table until it was all gone.

Now Uncle Richard's wife was Finnish. She could set before you a few US dishes that we were accustomed to, but her Finnish meals were really outrageous.

Finally, Uncle Cecil married an English woman. She, too, could cook English and a few US meals. However, her specialty was Mexican dishes. Surprised? Her parents came to America to teach in a small town in Colorado called La Junta. While in college, she worked for a popular Mexican restaurant where she worked up from a server to a cook. And mercy, did she have a wide array of authentic and delicious Mexican dishes and desserts.

My Aunt Mildred married a Bohemian. She had several specialties, but so did her hubby. At nearly every evening meal, the two presented a banquet of tasty delights. As usual, I was the last to leave the table.

Aunt Katheryn was married to an Englishman direct from the UK after WWII. He flew in the RAF during the war. After the war, he decided he needed a vacation to see the rest of the world. The vacation stopped abruptly when he met my aunt.

He wasn't a cook, but his mother left him all of his favorite recipes, which he turned over to my aunt. She became a terrific cook of wholesome and tasty English plates.

Darlene, my mother, was pretty good at satisfying a hungry appetite. She also began as a server in a Chinese restaurant and later became a backup cook. I can't recall all of the dishes' names except for one side dish, ham fried rice. My mother's second husband, a Bostonian, was pretty good at several Italian, German, Korean and Irish dishes, and he was also somewhat of a masterful mixologist.

Early in my youth, I spent time with a couple who became my very best friends. The woman was a descendant of the Aztecs, and her husband was Basque, who came directly from the north-western region of the Pyrenees. Breakfast came at 5:00 am and Dinner came anytime you were hungry. Like breakfast, both were FFY... Fend For Yourself meals. Lunch came at 11:00 am to 2:00 pm. This was the only fully prepared meal of the day. Several dishes included numerous variations of lamb, lamb stew, cod, Tolosa bean soup, sheep cheese and many other Basque delicacies. A Lunch usually was topped off with glass of a mild Basque cider and at least a one-hour siesta before returning to work.

Finally, I must include my wife in this array of International Family & Foods list. Although she is of French descent, in truth, she is an accomplished chef in the creation of many common ethnic and specialty recipes. Of-course, she is second to none when she pulls a delectable delight from her library of family recipes and... many of her own creations.

After what I have presented here, I believe I'm a bona fide International Family & Foods critic.

However, after a festival of tasty meals I often find it necessary to unbutton my tutu, use scissors to cut the buttons off my shirt just to relax my stomach's expansion. I never monkey around when I'm set before a well prepared and presented meal.

But ... I can still find, even in my state of fullness, room for a good ole stadium hot dog slathered with mustard and an ample amount of diced onions on top.

Remember, at 275 pounds, if I were ever to have the misfortunate experience of running into a bushy quilled porcupine, you won't want to be near me because after our paths cross, it certainly would be an ugly sight to see.

But that's the weight you have to bear when you are a bona fide International Family & Foods critic.

From Miami to Kansas

Coe Holden

My cousin in Kansas called and said, "Why don't you come and visit for a week?"

I answered back, "I can get away in about a week."

I made the arrangements and soon I was packing for the trip. I had never been to Kansas before, and it has been a long time since I saw my cousin. Bill had said to bring my coat. That's all he advised. Down here, all we wear are shorts, T-shirts, and sandals, so that is what I packed. It was sunny and 79 degrees in Miami.

I boarded the plane and was looking forward to a good visit with Bill and his wife Lynn. I was wearing pale blue shorts with thin stripes, a T-shirt, and sandals. This was a nonstop flight, so I settled down with a good book and saw little of anything out of the window.

When we arrived in Wichita, it was 13 degrees. I got off the plane and noticed some folks looking at me, but I didn't care or know why, must have been the way I dressed.

I got my bag and met Bill and Lynn. She snickered but said nothing. She just said she would get the car and left. Bill said I better put on my coat. I only had a windbreaker, so I put it on. That's all we need in Miami. Bill looked at me but said nothing.

Lynn was at the curb with the car. As I went to get in, I stepped in a snowdrift up over my ankles. Oh boy, was it cold. I sat in the back seat, shivering. Bill gave me his big coat, but I was still cold. We had to drive about an hour to Bill's place. They live in the country and heat with wood most of the time. They have a wood stove for heat, and I went to it as soon as we got to the house. It sure felt good.

Lynn went and got me a pair of Bill's long red underwear, a union suit with a trapdoor in the back. I put them on under my pale blue shorts; I was still in my sandals.

She started to laugh, and we all had a good laugh at my appearance. We kept on laughing even though I said it wasn't polite to l augh and point. I felt like I was getting warmed up, but not yet. Bill let me wear a pair of his boots. I still looked out of place.

Lynn asked me what size pants I wore and went to town and got me a pair of blue jeans. I soon looked like somebody instead of something of a transplant from another planet.

We did little except visit most of the week. It snowed almost every day.

Soon the week was gone, and it was time to leave for Miami. The sun was shining; it had warmed to 20 degrees. The wind was from the north and was freezing. When we got to the airport, I was wearing the long red underwear, blue jeans, T-shirt, and my sandals. Bill said to keep the underwear to remind me of the cold winters in Kansas.

When I got to Miami, it was 82 degrees. It didn't take me long to shed the long underwear. If I go back to Kansas, it will be in the summer.

It is so good to be home again.

A Childhood Dream Comes True

Bonnie Lacey Krenning

When I first saw an airplane flying in the sky as a child, I knew I wanted to be a pilot someday. I had many dreams, but this was one I held onto for a long time.

My husband, Bill, bought our Cessna 150 when we moved to our Park Place home in Wichita and kept it in a hangar at a small airport close to Wichita. We'd planned for both of us to learn to fly and get our pilot's licenses.

While checking around for my flight instructor, I heard about a young minister who had a good reputation for his students passing their test and getting licensed. Except he had never soloed one of his female students.

When I met him, his pleasant, respectful, and outgoing personality impressed me. He would accept me as a student, and I hired him on the spot. Thinking back, I wonder if he thought I would be another woman he would not solo and was just humoring me.

Bill had a heart attack when he was forty-seven—seven years before this—and recovered well. We found out that regulations required him to have a heart catheterization to get a pilot's license. He chose not to do that. I was relieved, because as a nurse, I had seen the procedure cause serious heart problems. In some extreme cases, death.

In reality, he was not as eager as me to become a pilot. He would grin and say, "I can climb as high as anyone as long as I can keep one foot on the ground." Eventually I realized he bought the plane for me, remembering how I had wanted to fly from the time I was a little girl.

It had excited me to start flying lessons, knowing nothing about an airplane except what I could see. My instructor showed me patience through all my many lessons.

Gradually, I became comfortable with take-offs and landings. We flew to other small airports doing "touch-and-go's," without stopping. I sometimes practiced stopping and taking off again. And I liked practicing climbing high until the plane stalled, then controlling the plane as it dropped and leveled off. My instructor had me doing maneuvers I might experience and teaching me how to regain control. It was all so exciting.

After I had taken many lessons, my instructor started saying, "When you solo—" and reminding me of previous lessons. One day, as we were landing, he said, "When you solo—"

I cut him off. "Oh, if you only knew how bad I want to solo!"

He looked surprised, maybe panicked. "Really?"

As I landed the plane, he said, "Pull over to the side and stop."

When we fully stopped, he climbed out of the plane, instructing me non-stop. I looked at him and I swear he was several shades paler than usual.

"Take the plane back on the runway and take it up," he said, a bit uneasily. "Circle around and do a touch-and-go."

My stomach fluttered in anticipation! I got back on the runway, fired up the engine, and took off again... by myself!

I flew back around and touched the runway. My instructor circled his arm in a motion for me to fly up again. After doing a couple more touch-and-go's, he motioned for me to pull over to the side of the runway and stop.

He ran toward me, laughing and shouting, "I could hug you!"

"I'm a hugger!" I hollered back. So, we hugged each other. But it wasn't over yet.

We got back in the plane and rolled over to our hangar and jumped out. He said with a smile, "When you solo for the first time, the custom is to cut off your shirttail and write the date you first soloed on it."

"I have worn this blouse for several weeks to 'sacrifice' the tail when I first soloed," I answered. I had already heard about this and was eager to do it.

He grinned. "We need some scissors."

"I have a pair in my purse." I had a short jacket over my blouse.

I grabbed my purse and quickly dug out the scissors. He took them and cut the back out of my blouse. The jacket covered the missing part of my shirt.

"We'll have to go to the office to get a pen to write on your shirttail."

I shook my head, smiling. "No! Guess what! I have a magic marker in my purse, too."

He took the pen I dug out of my purse, and he wrote today's date on my shirttail, and initialed it.

I was so excited that day I first soloed. And it was the first time my instructor soloed a woman. I hope it wasn't his last time.

Eager to get my pilot's license, I studied hard for the written test. My instructor referred me, and I took the test and passed it. He then referred me to a Designated Pilot Examiner (DPE) for my flight test. She worked at an airport on the east side of town. For the flight test, I flew our plane to her airport and landed.

She boarded the plane and had me do a take-off and a landing, also a couple touch-and-go's. Then she had me do a stall, which I did successfully. After that, she instructed me to fly back to her airport, land, pull over, and stop.

I sat there, heart racing in expectation, waiting for the wonderful words I wanted to hear.

She looked straight at me with a serious expression. "You are not ready to get your pilot's license. You need more practice with your instructor." Climbing out of the plane, she walked away without a backward glance.

I was heartbroken. I flew back to the airport where our plane was hangared, then drove home. Bill was away on his job.

Sobbing, I called my flight instructor, telling him how the DPE said I needed more practice.

"Hold on! I know you are ready for your flight test," he protested. "I know another DPE who will do the flight test with you."

He made the arrangements, and that DPE met me where we kept our plane. We climbed inside and he told me to roll out to the runway and take off, flying up into the sky. I did so, worried but confident.

He had me doing stalls and other maneuvers to test my ability to control the plane. One maneuver was tipping one wing down and flying around in a circle. He told me he was a stunt pilot, and smiling, suggested I may want to become one: a stunt pilot. I felt much better now.

After handling all the maneuvers well, he said, "You are ready for your pilot's license. I'll sign off for you to get it." He directed me to fly back to the airport.

When we landed, my instructor was waiting for us, excited for me.

It only took me forty-five years from the time I first saw an airplane flying in the sky and wanting to fly one myself. After getting my pilot's license, I often took my pre-school grandkids up flying in the morning. They may have thought all grannies took their grandkids in an airplane, just as we sometimes took them for a Sunday drive.

My sister's farm - Missouri
R. Tobey

That Special Night
Don Boldea

This story began many years ago. It happened during the last day and period of high school before graduation called Senior's week. You pretty much goofed off and irritated the heck out of the teachers.

Also, my class of study was bookkeeping, yuck! This class was mostly a boring double entry irritation. But I needed this elective course to graduate.

The teacher decided that we should spend our last hour sharing with the other classmates our after-graduation plans.

Being a smart-aleck, I asked if the teacher knew who Alice Cooper was. No, he didn't was his reply. So I started singing, "School's Out Forever" and my buddy, who sat behind me, chimed in. After the class finally began to quiet down, we were asked to sit down and refrain from any more of those kinds of disturbances.

We were always very respectful to all of our teachers and studied hard in all our classes all year long. But, Gene, my buddy and I decided since this was our last class of the day, and the last day of our high school experience, this was our day to celebrate.

Well, the next thing I know, he's accurately flipping paper wads to the back of our classmates' heads that were sitting around us, including mine.

Picture this. In this class there were no single desks, there were two person tables with seating for boy and girl partners. My buddy, the lucky stiff, sat with a partner who was a senior and a very pretty girl.

I sat in front of their table, and my partner was a junior. She was not as pretty as Gene's partner, but she wasn't ugly either. However, my partner had a squeaky voice that drove me nuts. Don't get me wrong, she was a sweetheart, intelligent and was a great help to me on all of our practice sets.

Anyway, Gene took great joy pelting me with paper wads.

One of them finally missed and landed in front of me on the table. I picked it up and tossed it over my shoulder. Gene started laughing, so I turned around to see what was so funny.

As he was laughing, he pointed to his partner. She was staring at me with a very harsh look on her face. Gene was pointing to his chest and then he slid his finger down to the opening of his shirt.

It seems my flip of the paper wad took a Don Drysdale errant like curve away from Gene and landed down the front of his partner's blouse. The realization of what I did caused my face to blush a bright reddish purple, and it was constrained in a peculiar form of terror.

After class I nervously waited in the hall to apologize for my childish conduct. When she appeared, I approached her and stuttered the most sincere apology that I could conjure up from my seemingly empty vocabulary archive. Graciously she accepted my clumsy apology. After we parted, I was finally able to form a well-meaning request for forgiveness. It was too late; she passed out of the building and climbed onto the waiting school bus. I tried to catch the bus, but it ran down the street like a go-cart super fueled by Taco Tico bean burritos.

Boy was she pretty. I'll never see her again. You big dummy, why didn't you talk to her and maybe offer to take her out for an apologetic pizza pie?

My mother asked who I was walking with at commencement. My answer was, "Hey mom, schools out forever. I'm not attending commencement." It became so quiet that you couldn't have heard a herd of trumpeting elephants as they tramped through a warehouse of bubble wrap.

When the moment passed, the first salvo she dropped was the guilt card. Then she tried the pride card and then, "please for me," card. If she had thrown out one more card of reason, I would have given into her request and said, "Okay, just for you, Mom."

The evening before graduation rehearsals I received a telephone call. A sensual voice said, "Hello! This is Joyce, remember me? I'm the catcher of your errant paper wad toss."

After a pause for composure, I answered, "Hi! How are you?

I am really ashamed and apologize." Her response was, "Oh, that's okay' or something like that. She continued, "Are you walking with anyone at commencement?"

I told her no I wasn't attending the happening. The next statement was, "That's too bad. I was calling to ask if you would be interested in walking with me in the procession."

Now I don't care what kind of games you play, but when a pretty girl asks if you would walk with her anywhere, that's a game changer for me. Trying not to sound too anxious, alright, I was like a hungry <u>tiger</u> pouncing on a swamp deer; I found myself immediately accepting the invitation.

I took her home after the ceremonies. I opened the car door and took her <u>hand</u> to assist her from the car. I kept ahold of her hand as we walked to her front door, yes hand in hand.

"Now, the rest of the story," is a segment Paul Harvey would articulate to end each of his radio commentaries.

She and I dated for a time after graduation and then went our separate ways. It was nearly a year later when one evening we accidentally ran into each other at a pizza parlor. We excused ourselves from our friends and sat at another table. A few moments later we left.

For some reason we ended up at the local municipal golf course on the ninth green. We lay out on a blanket and talked for hours. Suddenly the darn water sprinklers came on and we got soaked. That kind of drowned the romantic evening. But, before we left the green, I proposed.

Fifty-eight years of marriage later, we still reminisce about the unusual circumstances in which we met and my somewhat different proposal.

That truly was a special night.

Faith and Perseverance
Sherry A. Phillips

One winter a freezing rain made my driveway a Teflon ski slope. Up to the sidewalk and another rise before the flat concrete surface into the garage was a slick challenge for my Saturn sedan. A blowing snow added the possibility of staying stuck in the middle of the street where I had rolled after my first attempts to get home and in from the storm.

All but crawling up the hill on the grassy side, I slogged my way into the garage where I discovered "ice melt" crystals in a plastic jug with a handle and holes in the lid. On a shelf by the workbench, was five-pound bag of potting soil. Ah, tools for the task. I shook that jug of miracle melt balls out in front of me onto the icy concrete just like I shake salt on my eggs.

When the jug was empty, I crept back for the potting soil. Continuing my uneasy descent down the slippery driveway, I sowed handfuls of dry soil in a hefty arc out in front of me turning the ice black. I felt like I was throwing a sacrifice at the frozen feet of Old Man Winter. Handfuls of potting soil behind each tire was my last effort before trying again to ascend to safety.

Arms aching and fingers frozen, I pulled myself back into my snow-covered car. Inching backward then forward it was almost too easy to drive up those slopes and on into the now cold but dry garage. I put the Saturn in park and breathed a sigh of relief as the garage door rolled down. I was home. I was safe. I would soon be warm. I said a prayer of thanks to God. I was grateful I could see the help I needed was right there waiting for me.

In Kansas, as well as on my journey through life, ice and snow will freeze the landscape again and again. I can't always wait for it to melt on its own. Neither can you There are times we have to persevere until the sun shines again or life's challenges take a breather. Sometimes we have to make a choice when we come to a fork in the road. No matter which way we choose we do not know what lies ahead. But we can look around at the resources at hand. Recognize God equips us for the journey. Take courage. You do not travel alone and where you have the will there will be a way. Believe it!

Skinny Dippin'
Bonnie Lacey Krenning

It was fall, but I still wanted to waterski, and my husband was happy to let me. The water was warm and smooth. I tossed the skis into the water and got on them. To my delight, Bill pulled me around the lake for over an hour. He would smile back at me, watching for my signal to stop.

When I finally did, he pulled the boat over to the edge of the lake and turned off the engine. I handed up the skis and continued swimming around in the warm water. When I was a little girl, my brothers used to go skinny dipping on the farm. I'd never done that. Was this my chance to try it?

I looked around. There didn't seem to be anyone else in the area.

Excited and feeling daring, I stripped off my bathing suit while in the shoulder-deep water. As Bill looked at me and smiled, I tossed the suit up to him. He just grinned some more.

I floated, swam, and splashed around. Now I knew why my brothers liked skinny dippin'!

After a while, my curiosity was satisfied and asked Bill to throw me a towel. Still grinning, he did. I walked out of the water, wrapped in the towel, and climbed up the boat ladder straight into Bill's open arms. I expected us to head back to our cabin, where we would dress and go out to dinner.

Bill had other ideas. Always prepared for any situation, he'd already stocked the kitchenette with food. He asked me if I would like him to anchor the cruiser and spend the night on the lake. I eagerly agreed.

By that time, the sun had gone down, and it was dark outside. Bill put together enough snacks to make us a delicious meal, and we ate in the dim cabin lights. It had been a long, exciting day. We fell asleep snuggled in bed, rocking with the gentle waves.

The next morning, we went back to the cabin to eat breakfast and lunch there. We spent the remaining vacation days relaxing, fishing, skiing some more, and dining at the café in the evenings.

We had other vacations at Grand Lake, but none compared to that one alone with Bill when I got a little daring. There were no other skinny-dippin' times.

Camp Faculty Talent

E. L. Morrow

Back in the 1970s, I was directing a week of church summer camp for High School age. The conference had a traditional talent show on the next to the last night. Each cabin group and each learning group put together a talent entry. While the talent was mostly skits, a few were magic tricks or stand-up comedians. Also, it was a tradition for the faculty to participate by doing a skit.

The faculty consisted of cabin counselors plus learning group teachers. Cliff, my co-director, suggested our skit be a parody of a church choir. Being a religious group, everyone was familiar with both the positive and negative contributions of church choirs. Our goal was to include everything we could think of that is problematic about a church choir. We had the one who sang slightly off key, another always behind the beat, and of course, the deva who added a trill to the end of each phrase.

Cliff located some white robes sometimes used for commissioning services. Those became our choir robes. Taller people wore short robes, and shorter people had long ones that drug the floor. Each choir member had an oversized gaudy red bow made of construction paper and taped just below the collar. However, there was creativity in placing bows. One woman put hers in her hair, and one man wore his on his shoulder. As the director, mine was on my back, so when I turned around to direct, the audience saw the bow and the back of my head. We wanted to add a Walmart-style smiley face to the back of my head, but the idea came to us too late to implement.

By design, the directing appeared more like swatting flies than counting time for music. The direction rarely related to the rhythm of the music. Being in North Carolina, the song chosen was purported to be the state song: Pine Trees.

The words consisted of repeating Pine Trees thirteen times, sung to the tune of "Bless Be the Tie that Binds." The second verse is "Pinecones." You can add as many verses as desired as long as it begins with "pine," but it usually ends with a verse about "Pine Sap."

During the singing of the last verse, some choir members acted as if they had pine sap stuck to their fingers and spreading elsewhere.

Unknown to the director, one of the more popular campers organized a walkout during the second verse. So, when I turned to take our bow, only about six people remained instead of the eighty or so when we began.

But we got our revenge. The popular camper was a High School senior. They recruited him the next year as a junior counselor for a younger group directed by my friend Cliff. You guessed it, there was a faculty talent show skit, and he had to sing in the choir.

The moral is: don't mess with camp counselors. They have long memories and are patient.

Finding My "Sweet Spot"

Nancy Breth

A Tribute to C J (Cheryl Jeannette) Felton (11-20-53 to 12-6-16)

"One day your consciousness just opens up. You see life through a new lens. You see the best in everything; you see fresh new possibilities in your life. In other words, you see light at the end of the tunnel. You process your thoughts through new brain waves. Your thoughts come out positive, life affirming. Dreams take flight and your visions expand with wings of expression." From Peace is an Inside Job, by CJ Felton (pg xi).

March 2016

Out walking on a Sunday morning, I am thinking how glad I am that I listened to this restless child inside of me. This antsy child just wants to explore our wondrous world, not sit still on a church bench passively listening to Reverend Tim's messages. It's too confining and defining for me today. A beautiful sunny day is calling me to come out and play.

I enjoy Reverend Tim's inspiring words and especially his big hugs at the end of his services, but today I need that direct connection. That connection with God comes through loud and clear when I am outside walking, moving this stiff body of mine—flexing the muscles and the mind. Trying to find that "sweet spot" where I feel God's love flowing through me, letting that be my source of power.

I have reached a bridge overlooking a small stream. Then leaning over the bridge railing into this expansive view of Mother Nature's blessings. With no walls to obstruct my sight, I can see for miles, as if by leaning in, I have opened a door into another world. I enter a place where I feel very small, yet totally immersed and one with this whole huge ocean of love that enfolds me in this moment, here and now.

I let the cool breeze blow away these "should bees" buzzing around in my brain. As I am gazing out into "nothingness," a very ordinary-looking brownish-gray bird comes into view. She is flapping furiously, stirring my interest because she is having such a hard time getting lift-off and staying in the air. This small creature is flailing about as if she can't decide which way to go.

I wonder, "Is this a first flight, or is a gust of wind the cause of her erratic take-off?"

And then I see why. She has only half a tail, just one long tail feather. Her lopsided take-off is because of having only one rudder. I'm thinking she's going to crash to the ground any minute. But she doesn't give up; she keeps flapping her wings, and soon she is gliding along on a current so smoothly, flawlessly, that no one would know her body is damaged.

I follow her flight, amazed at this wee one's transformation from a furious flapper to a graceful glider. All the while knowing she had found that direct connection herself, that "sweet spot" where all she had to do was let go and let the unseen powers of Mother Nature take her higher.

Then my dear friend, CJ, comes into mind. The effects of ALS have ravaged CJ's body. Still, she refuses to give up and let the doctor's diagnosis and prognosis determine her flight path. For her, each new step in the progression of ALS is just another minor adjustment in her flight pattern. She keeps opening her mind and heart to the sweet possibilities God has in mind for her and gets back into that life-affirming stream of thought.

Since the diagnosis, she has published a book, written articles for various publications, still gives powerful, transforming workshops. Whatever she is doing, she has this beaming smile that lights up the whole room and the hearts of anyone nearby.

CJ has come to know the great joy that comes from being grateful. From loving everyone and everything that comes her way without complaint or needing for life to be different than it is. No matter how strong the winds blow that take her off course, she keeps getting back in alignment with the grace of God. Letting the jet stream of God's great love take her to a place of higher and higher consciousness.

Her life has been and will always be, an inspiring example to me of faith. Faith in a loving, lifting Universe. Faith in the possibilities when we remember we are each a miracle created by a loving god, here to love this wondrous life He gave us.

Yes, the winds blow, changing our bodies and surroundings in seemingly overwhelming and unbearable ways. And being human, we get off course. We have to flop around and change courses many times to find it, but that "sweet spot" is always there waiting for us to climb on board. Waiting for us to just get in alignment, lift our wings, and fly on the current of life—gliding gracefully, gratefully to all we were meant to be!

After December 2016

I can still see CJ flying down the street in her battery-operated wheelchair with her dog, Buddy, on her lap; headed to the neighborhood garden to harvest a few onions and green peppers. I ran to keep up with her the whole trip. And am still utterly amazed at her passion for life.

Someone once asked CJ (after being diagnosed), "How does it feel to be dying?"

And CJ answered, "I don't know; I am too busy living!"

Whenever I think of CJ, I ask myself, "Am I dying, trying, or flying?" Thanks to CJ's example, I know the answer is always my choice!

No Ticket Needed
E. L. Morrow

To understand my first train ride, I need to introduce you to my Uncle Charles. Charles Cash was married to my mother's oldest sister, Vischula. My mother was the youngest; there were twelve years between them. By the time I knew them, they were well-established. They had a house on a track of land, mostly wooded with a stream running through it.

By the time I was six, they had three adult children. The oldest was a teacher, one a water safety instructor, and the only one who remained at home was a civil engineer.

Uncle Charles' parents wanted him to become a lawyer. However, he wanted to do work with his hands. He liked outdoor life and saw himself working on the railroad. But he respected his family's authority.

The story goes his folks made him a deal: if he completed law school and didn't want to be an attorney, they'd give him the equivalent amount to do with as he pleased. They were sure he would like the legal profession if he gave it a chance.

He went to law school and graduated with honors. Receiving his diploma, he walked across the stage, down the aisle, took off his cap and gown, handing them and the diploma to his father. Leaving the campus, he walked several blocks to the railroad office and signed up to work at the switchyard in Charlotte, North Carolina.

The time I remember, Uncle Charles had seniority over everyone else, except one man—who signed up a few hours before him. They both wanted the same job: Switchman. Uncle Charles worked the night shift. He usually left for work about 9 pm for a shift starting at 11 pm.

Like most boys my age, I was crazy about trains. Uncle Charles was my hero because he actually worked on trains.

One summer, when I was six or seven, Uncle Charles arranged for me to go to work with him. Because I was a kid and not allowed to stay up all night, some other family members also went. They waited at the switchyard to take me back "home" at a "reasonable hour."

The job of the night crew at the switchyard was to put together the freight train that would leave the next day. During the day, the switch engines would go to the various factories and warehouses to collect the cars. For instance, a flour mill might have a shipment to go north to Philadelphia, another for Jacksonville, Florida, and one for Knoxville, Tennessee, all ready the same day. The day crew would pick up all three cars and park them on a siding.

There were three directions: north, south, and west. So, three different trains. When Uncle Charles came to work, he might find sixty cars sitting on eight to twelve different siding tracks to arrange on three different trains. Not only did they need to be going in the right direction, but they also had to be in the correct order; so that the last car was the one needing to be dropped off first, and then the next, etc.

I rode in the engine while they pulled from one to twenty cars down the track. My Uncle rode on the last car, hanging on to the ladder until they passed a switch. He would signal them with a flashlight, the engine would stop, he got off, turned the switch, or disconnected a car, or both. When ready, he would signal to them what to do next.

What I remember most about the ride was the importance of Uncle Charles' job. I also learned that you could send anything, almost anywhere on this continent, if a railroad went there.

My other vivid memory was how different it looks from the engine cab when viewing the stopped cars, with the crossbars down and the lights flashing. Riding in the train's engine was likely the best thing that happened to me that year. It would be forty years before I rode a train as a passenger.

Zip Up Your Tent!
Don Boldea

Ah! Spring is here again, the fresh new season of renewal. It's time to get the boys together for our annual fishing/camping trip. Our wives are taking their annual Caribbean spa/shopping trip so everybody is happy.

My buddy Mitch and I started this annual adventure eight years ago. We would pick a different state lake in a different state with a different kind of native fish to conquer. When we shared our exploits with our closest friends, the group of fishing/camping trip adventures grew to six.

Our transportation vehicles also grew. Our first vehicle was a simple, small, fuel-efficient SUV. Then we moved up to a medium-sized SUV as the group got bigger. The next size was a large fuel-gobbling SUV to satisfy the group's comfort. But, when it became a party of six, Mitch and I drew the line. We weren't buying an RV or a bus. So, we bought a four-by-six flatbed trailer and a trailer hitch.

The trailer would hold all our necessities and allow all the travel comforts possible inside the SUV. Plus, the trailer would permit the over-packing of some of our cohorts. This is where my nightmare begins.

Picture this: six tents, six sleeping bags, six large coolers, six different-sized duffle bags of clothes and toiletries, cooking pots, pans, plates, utensils, six camping chairs, an axe to cut firewood, one hundred feet of one-inch diameter rope, and a first aid kit.

I need to take a breather because I'm not done yet.

Finally, we needed a fish cooler to store the daily catch and ice. Now we load up the extra rods and reels and fishing tackle, three fish nets, numerous waterproof hip boots, and, of course, copious amounts of libation. Oh yes, one of our fellow fishermen, whose name we won't mention, but Billy found it necessary to bring his chemical toilet with a curtain surround. See what I mean? This was where the nightmare started.

After a long day's drive, we reach our destination, Ruby Lake. The lake is positioned at the foot of the Ruby Mountains that run vertically from the south to the north in eastern Nevada. This is the first lake Mitch and I fished; its clear, cold water gave up the most beautiful and delicious lake trout.

First things first, we need to find the secluded location Mitch and I initially camped. It took us nearly an hour before we rounded a small rocky outcrop, and there it was, just like we left it eight years ago.

Next we went to work setting up camp. Tents went up, and everyone was reminded to zip up their tent openings to keep out the nighttime varmints. Finally, the fire pit, comfortable camping chairs, and, yes, the bar were all set up.

Our first dinner consisted of campfire hamburgers, mustard, pickles, onions, potato chips, and a warm parka; the nights get a little chilly in the mountains.

Before relaxing from the long drive, dinner, and later retiring, the food containers were lashed together. We hung them high on a small tree limb a six-hundred-pound bear wouldn't dare climb. The bundle was then tied off with a rope out of a bear's reach. Lastly, the flatbed trailer was secured.

Everyone said goodnight and headed for their tent. Then Billy suddenly stopped and shouted, "Oh nuts my pink pillow has disappeared. Has anyone seen it?"

After a long rolling laugh from the rest of the gang, Mitch told him to look in the tire well of the SUV. "What a droll bunch of juvenile friends you guys are!" Billy said.

As we all unzipped and disappeared into our tents, a loud and continuous "Owwww" was suddenly heard. The yells of pain were coming from Billy's tent.

As the gang approached his tent he came out running around in circles, then back and forth, and then in circles again.

Following Billy of out his tent were several of those varmints that everyone was warned about. These creatures of the night had long pointy needles sticking out all over their bodies. The animals ran off into the dark while Billy kept dancing around with porcupine needles stuck in his derriere.

For over an hour, everyone took their turn pulling quills from Billy's body and smearing a whole tube of first aid cream into his wounds. The next day I took him to an emergency aid station in the small town of Elko below the lake. All was well.

Three days later, we broke camp. When we finished securing the flatbed trailer, Billy turned and said to the rest of us, "Thank you all for the fishing and comradery. But I have to say, this experience has exceeded all my worst nightmares. By the way, does anyone know where my pink pillow and commode are?"

This was a strange tale but true. However, when camping in Mother Nature's wonderland, you must always remember to keep your tent zipped up.

"I was praying for you, Mommy."
Bonnie Lacey Krenning

Spring came, and the summer went well after our move to Kirksville. Our kids liked their new yard. They could ride their pedal toys on the sidewalk, down the sidewalk, past the neighbors' houses. We bought Suzie a tricycle, so they each had a pedal toy. The neighbors were friendly and were pleased to have neighbors living there in the house.

That summer in town, we enjoyed our family's Sunday afternoon rides "in the country." Then we always stopped by the Dairy Queen. Bill and the boys each got a chocolate malt, and the girls and I each got a root beer float. At that time, the Dairy Queen only served outside, through a walk-up window. They closed in the fall, when the weather turned cold, until the following spring.

The house was clean and spotless when we moved in, a new experience for us. But it had not been redecorated for decades. I wanted to add my touch, so I papered the downstairs rooms, as I had learned to do at age thirteen, when I lived in Winchester, Kansas.

One day I decided to paper our stairway. It had a landing halfway up the stairway, then turned back on the other half to the upstairs floor. There was an ornate handrail beside the steps and across the upstairs hallway floor to the outer wall. I set a ladder on the landing. Then I placed a long twelve-inch-wide board from the ladder across to rest on the floor by the handrail at the upper hall's edge. Standing on the board and walking across it, I papered the stairway wall from the ceiling down to the steps' edge.

Our son, Charlie, was five years old. Shortly after I started papering that day, I noticed he was down on his knees on the upper floor, looking through the turnings of the handrail, watching me. He stayed there talking, sometimes asking questions, for over an hour. After I finished the last strip of paper, I got down and removed the board from the ladder.

He was quiet for a moment, then he said, "Mommy."
I answered, "What, Charlie?"
He softly said, "Mommy, I was praying for you."
What a sweet boy. That prayer may have saved me from falling, or worse.

The Moon Pie Tradition

E. L. Morrow

Back in my day, we had to walk to school. There was no bus service if you lived less than two miles from school. We lived less than a mile from Fern Creek Elementary School. I always thought it was a strange name for a school. Central Florida had no creeks—lots of lakes, but no creeks. And no ferns anywhere near the school. So why did they name it Fern Creek? Maybe it was named for a person. I'll have to check that out. But I digress. Where was I? Oh yes.

Back in my day, we walked to school. When I was in sixth grade, my sister was starting first grade. So, for a year, I got to walk to and from school with my little sister. The following year, I was in junior high, and she was still in elementary. So, it was only one year that we went to the same school.

I wouldn't say we were poor, but to my father, paying a dollar twenty-five a week for school lunch was "highway robbery." So, we took our lunches from home.

As it happened, the first graders' lunch ended as my class arrived at the lunchroom. Those who brought lunch to school entered by the exit door and went to our assigned tables. After the first few weeks, my sister and I started the tradition of sharing the moon pie.

Back in my day, the moon pie was all the rage as dessert for kids. If you have never seen one, it's round—shaped like the moon. They made it of two graham cracker circles held together by a marshmallow center and completely coated in a waxy chocolate shell.

Well, as I said, we weren't exactly poor. To prove it, we would get a box of twelve moon pies each week at the grocery store. It was my family's idea of a luxury desert. My father also took his lunch six days per week. Since he was bigger, he got a whole pie each day. That left one to be divided each day between the two of us. I think mother ate the twelfth one.

Back in my day, they considered a pocketknife almost a necessity for boys. A few years later, when switchblades became a problem, the school banned all knives. But that year, I carried my single-blade knife used only for the moon pie or occasionally whittling a stick into a pointed stick. I don't know why we thought sticks needed points, but I digress again.

Back to the tradition. My sister had permission to leave her class table and come to my spot. I had the moon pie in my lunch, the pocketknife in my back pocket, along with my wallet, which contained no money but a picture of Hopalong Cassidy. That's another story.

My sister arrived at the table. I would ceremonially remove the moon pie from my lunch bag. Take it out of the cellophane wrapper. Get out my knife, open the blade, wipe it with a napkin, and cut the moon pie. My goal was to cut it into precisely two equal pieces. Because the rule was "I cut—you choose."

My sister would pick her piece and eat it. I had to put mine back in the wrapper to be eaten after my sandwich and piece of fruit. Before the rest of my class got through the serving line and came to our tables, my sister's class was gone.

That was one of many ways my folks made ends meet. But while doing so, they gave us a bit of luxury and created a fond memory, back in my day.

Ugly Green Car

Donald Grabendike

It was the spring of 1955, school was almost out, and it was time to think about Sleepy Hollow Park with trees, the creek, and most importantly, the fun that lay ahead. But there was one problem. We had moved. Not just down the street, but over a mile away. New house, new school, new friends, and no Sleepy Hollow. What a bummer! How was I to enjoy summer vacation without my beloved park?

Then one evening at the dinner table, father asked, "Would you," (you being me, an overactive 12-year-old), "like to build a Soap Box Derby Car?"

I had heard of the Derby, but that was it. The word BUILD was something I understood. I really don't think Father was trying to make up for my loss of the park, but rather he was looking forward to the challenge.

It was agreed upon, a fine car is what we would build. Phase one became my mother's responsibility. She was to take me to the Chevrolet dealer to register for the race and purchase a set of axles and wheels. A young racer could not use just any wheels. Oh, no, they had to be official Soap Box Derby wheels, and Chevrolet was the national sponsor.

So, one day after school, we jumped in the car and headed out to get a set of rules and register for the big race. When we arrived at the dealership, I climbed out of the car and took off on the run to declare my intentions to become a racer. I went to the counter clutching my money, and with wide eyes, I told the lady standing there that I wanted to enter the Soap Box Derby.

She looked down at me, smiled, and said, "I'm sorry you can't register here. You must go to the other Chevrolet dealer, and they are just down the street."

Back to the car, and we went down the street. When we got there, Mom went in with me. I paid my money for the wheel kit, then filled out the registration form she signed, giving her permission for her little boy to go zooming down some hill in search of fame and fortune. Fame, being my picture in the newspaper and fortune, a Cushman motor scooter.

Father and I sat down that evening after dinner and looked at the rules. According to the pamphlet, the race car had to use the official wheels, have a functioning brake, and a steering wheel that would move the front axle in either direction, but only two inches. There was another very important rule which I will go into detail later.

A week later, we started on the car. The rules stated the boy was to build the car himself with the assistance of an adult. Notice I said "boy." In those days, no one even thought of letting little girls race cars. My, have things changed.

Anyway, we were off to the races, so to speak. We would go down to the lumberyard each Saturday and work on my car. We would cut boards, drill holes, sand, and sand. I can understand Father letting me drill holes and sand, but for him to allow a 12-year-old to run a table saw, and radial arm saw was unbelievable, but I did.

After several Saturdays, my race car started to take shape, and it was time to put the final touches on the body. Father had worked at Cessna, had a good working knowledge of aerodynamics, and had designed a body with compound curves on both the front and rear decks. This was great, but it called for more cutting and sanding. Part of the sides and top were made from narrow strips of plywood, attached to several curved bulkheads, and gaps were filled with plastic wood.

At first, I tried to put the plastic wood on with a putty knife, but shortly I went to scooping up a big blob between two fingers and smearing it onto the body. This technique worked swell and went fast until the putty dried, not on the car but on my fingers. Do you know how long it takes to remove plastic wood from your fingers? Days. It was easy to put it on the car and get it off my fingers. The hard part was sanding it down to get it smooth. I sanded and sanded, but we were running out of time. The race was the following weekend, and we had to get it painted.

Once again, it was time for Mom to help. She got a brush and some paint, and I slopped it on. That is the best way I can describe my painting skills.

My friend Lyle lived down the street and was also building a car. His car was low and sleek, and it had a sheet metal body and a shiny coat of paint, which was beautiful! Fortunately, no one had seen my car because I built it at the lumberyard and didn't take it home until just before the race.

When race weekend arrived, Father loaded my car up on the big lumber truck on Friday and brought it home, ready for the car inspection and trial run on Saturday. The following morning, we headed downtown, but first we had to stop at Lyle's house to pick up his car.

Lyle and his dad rolled his car out of the garage, and we loaded it up on to the truck. By this time, there were several little boys around, all eager to view this display of fine racing machines. There they sat. Lyle's pretty car and my big ugly green thing. They all poked fun at my car, but I didn't care. I was going to be a race car driver.

When we arrived at the inspection headquarters, several men were there to help unload the cars and get them in line for the inspection. At the first station, two men would check the outside dimension to ensure that they were within the rules. I then rolled my car to the next station, where I climbed into the car to demonstrate my ability to steer the big hunk of wood. They gave me a big push, and after about fifteen feet, I applied the brake to bring her to a stop. It worked. Yea!

Now, only one more inspection. The scales. Remember me telling you earlier about the important rules? Well, the one that I didn't talk about was weight. No car and driver could weigh more than 250 pounds, and I was looking right at the scales. They rolled me and the car onto the scales, and I watched the needle swing around and stop. 249 and ½ half pounds. I made it! I passed the inspection. All I had to do was make a trial run, and I would be ready for the big day.

The next morning, our whole family went to the track with me, dressed in a white official Soap Box Derby T-shirt and a pressed paper crash helmet atop my head. Oh, I was excited!

The men helping the day before had arranged the cars in numerical order at the top of the hill. All I had to do was walk down the line to find my car. You are probably thinking, where in the heck could they find a hill tall enough in Kansas to hold a gravity-powered race? The Kellogg overpass. Can you imagine closing US Highway 54 in both directions for two days? They did in the 1950s.

And then it was time. They played the national anthem over the loudspeakers, and then the announcer said, "Gentlemen, return to your racers."

Picture this: 200 plus little boys from all over Kansas and parts of Oklahoma, kneeling beside their cars. They propped each car up on oil cans with its driver putting drops of oil in the wheel bearings, followed by a brisk snap of a rag to get the wheel spinning. Oil and spin, spin and oil. This was going on everywhere you looked.

It wasn't long before I heard my friend Lyle's number called. It was time for his first run. He won, so that meant that those men in the shiny new Chevy pickups would bring him and his beautiful, sleek car back to the top of the hill, and I was there to congratulate him.

After what seemed like forever, I heard my number called. I carefully pushed my car to the starting platform, turned it over to the officials, and climbed up to the top. The men quickly placed my car and one beside me on the starting ramp, with the noses resting on steel plates that kind of stuck up out of the floor. Then we each wiggled into our cars, awaiting the countdown. Three, two, one, GO!

We were off. We went down the ramp with a thump and bump; the cars rolled onto the concrete. At first, we rolled slowly, not more than a good walking pace, and then the slope got steeper, and we began going faster.

The finish line was almost a block away, allowing gravity to do its work. With each second, the bumps in the concrete got closer until it was bumpety, bump and the checkered flag was in sight.

Then it happened. The flag went down, and it was on my side. I won!

The race crew quickly loaded my car onto the awaiting pick-up, I climbed in, and away we went to the top of the hill. By this time Lyle was in line for his second race of the day, waiting his turn. The green flag came down, and he was off. Another win.

Then it was my turn. Down the ramp to the finish line, get the checkered flag, no problem. Hooray for team Pinecrest! We both lived on Pinecrest Street.

When it came time for the third race, Lyle was not so lucky, and now the reputation of our team was left to me. When it was my turn, I won again and again. I don't know exactly how many times I went down the hill on that Sunday afternoon in July, but it was a lot.

Finally, there was only one race left, the race between the junior division and the senior division. I had won the 11- and 12-year-old group and a kid named Sonny had won the 13- and 14-year-old division.

Now it was time for the big race. The race to determine the overall winner, the fastest car at the track. When the green flag went down, and we rolled down the track, we were neck and neck.

Down the hill, past the cheering crowd, toward the finish line, I have that white car next to me all the time. I could see him out of the corner of my eye, and he was not gaining on me, but neither was I on him.

Then finally we were approaching the finish line. I could see the flagman standing tall with the flag in hand, then I saw it come down, not in my lane but the one beside me. I lost.

I may have lost the race, but I got my moment of fame when the Wichita Eagle newspaper published a picture of me with my car. As far as the fortune, Sonny won the motor scooter, a trip to Akron, Ohio, to the national race, and I won a small gas-powered race car. When I discovered I couldn't fit into the race car, I sold it. I bought a portable typewriter and a battery-powered radio. But the best part of my winnings was the admiration I received from my friends who, only a short time before, had made fun of the big ugly green car.

Over the years, I have had several close calls with the first-place award until, in 1966, I won first place at the BATTLE OF BEAR TRAP RANCH.

The Magic in a Photograph
Starla Criser

I'm a collector of many things, including teapots, fun little birdhouses, unique wooden bowls, or vases, and much more. All to the dread of my daughter—a minimalist, who will one day inherit them. That is her problem, not mine. She can sell or give away whatever she wishes. But I treasure my collections and will continue to add to them until the day I pass on.

Another of my collections—the biggest one—is my photos. I have well over 11,000 photographs saved in iCloud, a considerable number of scanned in old photos, and a half dozen photo scrapbooks. I really enjoy being able to take a vast number of pictures on my phone wherever and whenever I choose. That capability is leaps and bounds past the days of using a camera with film. You had to take at least several pictures of whatever you were trying to capture, just hoping that one of them would turn out when you got the film developed.

Now I can sit in a comfy chair and thumb through my albums. Or flip through my library in the Photos app on my laptop. With my printer, I can also print off my favorites, frame them, and set them around my house or hang them on the walls. I'm in photo heaven!

There is such "magic" in a photograph. Each one can tell so many stories and bring so many memories back.

Sometimes I let my daredevil side out. I will never feel defined by my age. As long as I am able, I will try new experiences. And I recall them best when I run across a photo of the event.

One of my "daring" experiences happened while on vacation in Maui with my husband, daughter, son-in-law, and his parents.

I had always wondered what it would feel like to go ziplining. My son-in-law, Jason, indulged my interest and took me, and his mother, Glenda, to Lahaina, where we all climbed up to the high platform. With the help of a guide/instructor, they put us into safety harnesses, put on helmets, and told us to hang onto the rope above our heads. We could let go with one hand and take pictures with our phones hanging around our necks. On the incredible glide down the lines, I could spin around take as may pictures as I wanted. I took a lot! I wasn't the least bit worried about zipping through the air, hanging by a cord. Glenda absolutely did not release her two-handed grip on the rope to take pictures. It was a wonderful experience, and I can't wait to try it again somewhere else.

Another memorable time was when my husband and daughter went with me to Italy. My husband, Steve, thought he was special driving our rented care on the famous autostrada (superhighway) with its speed limit of 80 mph, which was basically ignored as other cars whipped by us. I have many favorite photos from that trip, but it makes me feel good when I look at the photo of Steve, wearing one of his berets, driving in Rome. He loved driving that car, even if he got a ticket near the Leaning Tower of Pisa. Long story, funny too.

Then there was the time my daughter, Angela, and I traveled to the United Kingdom. We rented a car and drove from the end of England to Scotland, Wales, and even Ireland. So much fun! This was before the fancy GPS systems, when we used a combination of odd maps on our phones and a paper map. If you think using maps like that in the United States was tricky, it's nothing like using them in another country.

On that trip, we headed down from Inverness to where we would stay the night in Wales, far south. Halfway there, we realized we had missed seeing Loch Ness near Inverness. We couldn't miss that! What if we missed seeing the Loch Ness monster? So, we drove back, and while I got some great pictures, Nessie failed to make an appearance.

On another trip with my daughter, we went to France and drove around, including going to Paris. Who could miss going there and seeing the Eiffel Tower, the Seine River, and so much more? I have many photos of the Eiffel Tower, which are beautiful. But one of my favorite photos in Paris was of the famous Pont des Arts, also known as the Lock Bridge. Visitors attached personalized padlocks to the railing and threw the keys into the Seine River. Since we traveled there, they have removed over 40 tons of "love padlocks" for safety reasons. But it was fun to see that site.

I could go on and on discussing my favorite travel photos and their meaning to me. Instead, I will talk about a few of the family photos that touch my heart.

One slightly faded photo is of my husband, myself, and our daughter on Halloween in 1982. Angela is wearing a blue Smurf costume. Steve and I are wearing outfits I made. I'm dressed in a super baggy clown costume with face makeup. Steve is adorable in a pudgy snowman costume, complete with a corn cob pipe, hat, and face makeup. I still have those costumes, but I can't talk Steve into wearing his outfit again.

Another fun memory photo is of my mother-in-law, Letha, sitting on "Santa's" lap. Her youngest son, Terry, wore the Santa costume, much to the delight of some older aunts and uncles during the special time together.

I can't forget another favorite photo of my mother-in-law. Steve and I were living in New Mexico when my in-laws came to visit us. We went fishing, and the family was not known for being fishermen. The picture shows Steve, his dad, and Letha grinning as she holds up this small fish she'd caught. She was so proud.

Remember the Twister game? I have a picture of my barefoot dad trying to play the game, which he loved. He loved games of all kinds, especially card games. He was always a jokester, teasing us when we tried to put puzzles together by hiding the last piece.

I can't leave out favorite photos of my mother. I'm not what you would call "athletic," but Mom was even less so. Still, she tried things. I have a picture of her posing with a friend with their tennis racquets. I don't remember her playing tennis more than once or twice. There is also a photo of her jumping up and down on one of those mini trampolines. Her smile always makes me smile to look at her.

As I said earlier, photographs are special; looking at them can bring back such treasured memories. I plan to take at least another 10,000… maybe more.

My Favorite Christmas Tree
Bonnie Lacey Krenning

From the first time I saw a Christmas tree in my one-room school, I have enjoyed having and decorating my own Christmas tree. Over many decades, my Christmas trees got bigger and bigger. My husband, Bill, always helped me, sometimes reluctantly, get the live trees I wanted.

After our kids were grown and settled in their own homes, I still wanted a live tree. The day after Thanksgiving, I again coaxed Bill into taking me to get one for us and haul it home in his pickup. We brought the tree home, and he built a sturdy stand and secured the tree to it. It nearly reached the ten-foot ceiling in our front room.

Bill set the tree in our large bay window. To be sure the tree was stable, he tied two ropes in the middle of the tree's trunk and fastened the ropes to window latches on opposite sides. As the limbs settled down, the ropes were barely noticeable. The tree filled the window area. Now, the decorations….

In late summer, I started a plan for a new set of decorations. I bought foods I could use in six-ounce cans, and when they were empty, turned them into little lanterns. I cut large "windows" in each can's sides and lined them with sheets of transparent, colored plastic. I made domed roofs from soft sheets of aluminum for each lantern and fastened each to a large tree light. There were about one hundred lanterns.

With the help of a ladder, I started putting them on our Christmas tree. As the branches settled, the lights had to be adjusted. With the lanterns and all the decorations I collected over the years, it loaded the tree down. It was the biggest and most beautiful tree I/ we ever had.

Everyone seemed to enjoy the tree that could be easily seen in the bay window. Even the mailman knocked on the door one day and asked to come in to see our Christmas tree. Our kids and their families dropped by more often. We also invited my extended family, who came for a Sunday dinner Christmas party and stayed until evening. Neighbors and friends from our church dropped in. The tree was much enjoyed.

We usually took our Christmas tree down by New Year's Day. After putting so much fun and effort into decorating it that year, I was reluctant to take it down. Then…

One evening, I heard Bill come in the front door from work. When he didn't walk on in, as usual, I walked up front to meet him. He was standing, looking at the Christmas tree, then he looked at me. In a soft, firm voice, he said, "If you don't take that tree down, I'm gonna quit comin' home."

When I thought about it, I realized the date. It was February 15.

I was a little stunned, but not too surprised. I don't think Bill meant it, but I didn't take any chances. I took my favorite Christmas tree down the next day. Still, my biggest and most beautiful Christmas tree had been worth it all.

A Curly Porcupine
Mary Denney

This is my first/worst nightmare. When I was about eleven years old, our family had moved to a small town west of Wichita, Kansas. I have never been comfortable moving, but this move was especially difficult. Our new house was brand new and had beautiful hardwood oak floors.

It was a small-town school with all twelve grades in one building. My sixth-grade class had fifteen children, and we shared a room and teacher with about ten fifth graders, which made maybe thirty kids in the room. The school had one music teacher who went from room to room throughout the day. The whole town had about 275 families, and everything centered around the school.

One day, the music teacher came to our class and explained that the PTA (Parent Teacher Association) had asked for a musical program for their Christmas meeting. She wanted a triple trio, a trio, a quartet and a solo, and each was to learn a song and perform. She asked for a show of hands of those willing to be in the triple trio. Several hands went up. Then she selected people to perform in each of the musical groups until she came to the solo. No one lifted their hand. She was getting angry and insisted that someone had to raise their hand!

Now I was an especially shy child and in a totally foreign environment, I was torn between her anger and my fear of what to do. I didn't know what a solo was, but if it would appease her anger, I decided I must do it. I meekly raised my hand, and she turned, all smiles. She had her victim.

The next day she told me I would be singing "Frosty the Snowman" and asked if I knew it. Yes, I did, and I decided it might turn out okay. Little did I yet know that I would sing it all by myself, in front of the entire town. That night I told my mother what I was going to be doing, and she was quite happy with me, too. She told me she was going to get me a new dress to wear for it and it would be my

Christmas present. Then I asked her what a solo was.

That night was my first/worst nightmare. Those beautiful oak floorboards turned into snakes and were crawling all over me. I must have been screaming and crying and the next thing I knew, I was in the bed with my parents. My father held me close and with my head safely on the pillow, the thought of a new dress made the horror grow dimmer. All by myself? What a pickle.

In a small town, even the old folks walk over to the school to see the Christmas program at the December PTA meeting. I felt like the whole town was there and had flooded into the gymnasium. I can still remember singing that song seventy years later. And the navy-blue jumper and white blouse. My pink parka protected me as I walked to the school.

Bless her heart, my mother was determined to show her daughter to advantage. She gave me a home permanent and curly hair. Try to imagine a porcupine with curly quills. They stuck out of my head like little cork screws. All I can say is I was a very brave little girl. My mother went to cosmetology school and became a licensed beautician.

Lessons from My Cat, Mandi

Dianne Waltner

"I have studied many philosophers and many cats. The wisdom of cats is infinitely superior." - Hippolyte Taine

Over the course of my life, I've been fortunate to have had the opportunity to learn from some of the world's greatest teachers: cats. And I continue to learn from my cat Mandi, who has lived with me for over thirteen years. We don't know for sure how old she is since I adopted her from the Kansas Humane Society as an adult stray. The vet estimates her to currently be around sixteen, which classifies her as a "super senior" cat, with an approximate age of 80 for humans.

I adopted her at a low point in my life, after losing my mother, when I was struggling with thoughts of suicide. I knew that if I adopted her, I would honor the commitment to care for her for life. She gave me a reason to live and provided companionship. Some days when I didn't feel I could get out of bed, she would curl up next to me. Feeling her sleeping by my side was very comforting, reminding me that I wasn't alone. And providing me with the motivation to get up to feed and care for her. I felt that everything would be okay.

We've had several health scares over the years, and I was terrified that I would lose her in 2013. It was a very stressful year with a lot of vet appointments, specialty vet appointments, and emergency vet visits. But, with lots of love and care, she survived and has gone on to live a generally happy, healthy life (which will hopefully continue for several more years).

Like me, there are days when she acts (and seems to feel) as though she's aging. But there are other days when she still displays her more kittenish side, racing frantically from one room to the next and jumping effortlessly onto the back of the sofa. Those days are getting fewer, however. But I continue to enjoy her company immensely and remain open to the lessons she's trying to teach me. These are just some of the things I've learned through our time together:

1. Remain curious throughout life. You never know when you'll discover something new.

2. There are always new things to explore and new ways of looking at life.

3. Sometimes it helps to get a new perspective or vantage point.

4. It never hurts to ask for what you want—you may just get it. You'll never know if you don't ask. And, even if you don't, nothing is lost.

5. Express your feelings. Don't keep them bottled up.

6. Speak up when you have something to say. Don't be afraid to be heard.

7. Don't get too set in your ways. Remain open to new possibilities and opportunities.

8. Remember that it's never too late to try something new.

9. Be persistent. Sometimes it takes more than one (or several) attempts to get what you need.

10. Take time to bask in the sunshine.

11. Don't forget to stretch.

12. Napping is good. It's okay to rest.

13. Breakfast is important.

14. Play is vital at all ages.

15. Don't let your age dictate what you can (or can't) do.

16. Be unpredictable - keep surprising everyone.

17. Pay attention to what's going on around you.

18. Take time to enjoy the natural world. Watching birds and squirrels is fascinating.

19. Sometimes it's good to retreat to a safe place where you can tune out the world.

20. Forgive quickly and often.

21. Don't hold grudges.

22. Sometimes listening is the most important thing you can do.

23. Live in the moment. Don't stress over the future.

24. It's okay to just sit and contemplate. We don't have to be busy all the time. Busyness is overrated.

25. Perhaps most importantly: Don't hesitate to show your affection and let people know you love them. This life is short; we never know which day will be our last.

I love Mandi dearly and am so very grateful for her. She's been an important part of my life, and I cherish each day with her.

Go Granny Go
Nancy Breth

August 2002, Corpus Christi, Texas

My grandson Alley (Albert) and I were getting tired and cranky after a long hike along the beach. So, Grandma Nancy decided it was time to go back to our motel room, leaving my son and daughter-in-law at the beach for alone time.

Grandma had visions of showers to cleanse our bodies of sand caked in every crevice. And a relaxing nap with the cool air soothing our bodies after our long walk in the burning hot sun.

But four-year-old Alley took one look at the motel pool and forgot all about the quiet time we had promised Mom to do before pool time.

I bribed him with, "OK, Alley, you don't have to take a nap first; but you have to take a shower."

The only way I could get him to take a shower was to get in with him—still in my swimsuit.

As soon as I got him all toweled off, he was ready to race outside to the pool in the buff. It was like trying to catch a greased pig; but I managed to pull on his wet suit while he was struggling to get out the door. I forgot that "wait" is one of those "no-no" words in a four-year-old's world.

After the fifth "Wait for Grandma," I discovered the safe latch at the top of the door that opened to the outside sidewalk.

I was feeling oh-so-on-top-of-this-now as I went back to the shower, pulled off my cold, wet bathing suit and climbed into the warm shower. After the fastest shower I have ever taken, I grabbed a towel and patted off the large drips. I played tug of war with the wet suit, getting it up and over my lower half, when I heard the door to the outside open and Alley's squeal of delight.

In full frontal nudity, I peeked out of the bathroom just in time to see him racing toward the pool as a couple walked past the wide-open door.

I ducked back in the bathroom, stuck my head around the corner and pleaded with Alley to come back in. He just laughed at me, feeling so clever at getting himself free.

I grabbed a towel quickly to cover my top and ran to the door to drag him back inside before he got to the pool gate. And before anyone else saw this grandma in distress.

My first thought was to be the stern parent and give a lecture because he had disobeyed; but then I remembered. I am a grandparent. My job is to enjoy this child.

I looked into those big blue eyes, full of excitement and visions of things to see and do. And I saw the joy of this moment lighting up his face.

So instead of the lecture and berating him for being so clever in stumping Grandma, I laughed so hard tears streamed down my face.

This time, though, I dragged him into the bathroom with me, securing the door while finishing wriggling into my bathing suit.

"OK, Grandson, I'm ready now!

"Lead the way, Alley. Help me see and live the world through your eyes now. Another chance to live each moment as you do; eager for the next," I said to the whirlwind he created racing to the pool.

Never Forget
Mary Denney

We have experienced historical events in our lifetimes that will never be forgotten in history. Today I am commemorating three. Two will be in the history books for future generations to read about and perhaps wonder what it would have been like to witness these events. One is personal to me, but connected to one of the other two events.

First is the attack on the World Trade Centers in New York City, on September 11, 2001. Every one of us can recall vividly where we were and how it felt as this historical event unfolded.

I was at work on the eighth floor of the Olive Ann Garvey Building, 200 West Douglas, in Wichita, Kansas, when my youngest daughter Valerie, called me and said, "Mama, an airplane has just crashed into the World Trade Center, in New York City." She was a new student at WSU (Wichita State University) and hadn't left for school yet. As she was explaining what they were saying on the news, she gasped and said, "Oh no! Another plane has crashed into the second tower, and they are saying we are under attack!"

As that day progressed, the world as we knew it changed. Every aircraft in the United States was instructed to land at the nearest airport, and air travel has never been the same. They instructed foreign aircraft not to land in our country. A fascinating novel, The Day the World Came to Town – 9/11 in Gander, Newfoundland, by author Jim DeFede, tells the story of one such aircraft.

I walked across the hall and told attorney, Faith Maughan, about it and she tuned in on her computer to the story. Soon her office was full of others in the law firm, all of us aghast at the events that followed. Next, the Pentagon was hit and then an aircraft crashed in Shanksville, PA. None of us knew what might happen next. We were on the eighth floor!

At noon that day, I left the law office and went home for lunch. I immediately noticed a strange silence. There were no airplanes in the air. There wouldn't be any for days on end. When I returned to the building after lunch, the building was locked. I had a fob and could enter the building and return to work. Later, we learned that the entire downtown had locked down. We also learned that a large contingent of Japanese businessmen was at a meeting in Century II across the street from our office. No one knew who was responsible for the reprehensible events.

2,750 people died at the trade centers, 343 Firefighters lost their lives, 184 died at the Pentagon and forty died in Shanksville, as they thought their airplane to be headed to the White House in Washington DC.

The second event, my own dearly departed brother, Ted Trask, his son Scott Trask, and son-in-law, Derek Davis, went to New York City for a Ceremony Commemorating Firefighters not long after 9/11. All three were Wichita Firefighters. Ted worked for the Wichita Fire Department for forty years and retired as Battalion Chief. His son is a Captain, and his son-in-law is a Lieutenant. Ted was born on September 14, 1949, and died on my birthday, December 21, 2021, of complications following an aorta transplant. Ted recently told me his greatest achievement was not to lose one firefighter while he was in command. Well done, good and faithful servant!

The third historical event is the death of Queen Elizabeth II. The longest serving Queen in England's history. Seventy years on the throne, the history books will include her ninety-six-year-old life story.

Our Siamese Cat
Bonnie Lacey Krenning

One Sunday afternoon, a couple of weeks after Bill and I met, we were riding down the street in his '31 Model A. A black cat ran across the road in front of us. Bill swerved as though he was going to hit it, causing the cat to scamper away. I yelled, "Stop! Why would you do that?"

He seemed embarrassed and surprised at my yelling and said, "I was just playing. I would never have hurt it." I accepted he meant it, but it took a while for me to relax.

Years later, after we were married and living in the country, our kids brought stray cats into the house and made them pets. Bill disapproved of having cats in the house. He thought animals, especially cats, should not be inside.

In Wichita, our kids soon "acquired" a calico cat and a small dog for pets. They always took good care of their pets, making sure they fed them. Even though we didn't have a tomcat or a male dog, they usually had litters a couple of times a year. Once, both of our cats and our dog had litters at the same time. Altogether, we had twenty-one pets in the house. We were always able, though, to place the puppies and kittens into good homes.

Soon it became known our kids had a way with cats. One evening our next-door neighbor knocked on our back door. He told me while he was at work someone left a cat in his car. When he tried to get the cat out of his car, it clawed and scratched him. Our neighbor knew our kids liked cats and asked if they could coax it out of his car.

After some time, our kids coaxed the cat into their arms and brought her to our house. She soon made herself "at home," but Bill wasn't pleased to add another cat to our collection of animals. She was a full-blood Siamese cat, so I named her Malacca, after a city in Siam.

Malacca didn't accept Bill's apparent rejection of her. One day, while he sat at the dining table in his captain's chair, I saw Malacca edging her way toward him, rubbing his legs, then she jumped up into his lap. She gently nipped at his arms and hands until he petted her. He let her stay in his lap, and she went to sleep. As time went by, she often repeated the routine while he ate, watched TV, or read the paper.

Add to that…. When Bill settled into bed at night, he would stretch out on his back, cross his long legs, and pull the covers up over his arms. He folded his arms across his chest and slept like that most of the night. Malacca would sometimes crawl up on the bed and sleep on his chest…. and he would let her stay there.

One night, when I was sound asleep, Bill awakened me by loudly hollering, "What the hell?" He quickly threw the covers back, and I heard Thunk! Thunk! Thunk! Getting up, I slid my feet on the floor until I reached the light switch. Turning it on, I saw newborn kittens on the floor, five of them! I gathered them up and put them in Malacca's bed. She did have a bed.

This is a true story! I swear! Do you think Bill's claim that he didn't like cats was true? Not!

CONTRIBUTORS

CONTRIBUTOR LIST

AUTHOR/TITLE	LOCATION

AUTHOR/TITLE   LOCATION

Our Continuing Project

The continuing project focuses on publishing writing collections from members of the Wichita, Kansas senior centers.

Write On, published in 2017, is a collection of stories, memoirs, and poems from 23 Wichita area authors.

Write Again, published in 2018, is a collection of stories, articles, memoirs, and poems from 29 Wichita area authors.

Daring to Share, published in 2019, is a collection of poetry, thoughts, and short stories from 35 Wichita area authors.

All the collections are available online at Barnes & Noble and Amazon. They are also in the Wichita library.